The Critics on Edna O'Brien

'Edna O'Brien's imagination inflames the world'
Independent on Sunday

'Exquisitely written, with glowing descriptions of the natural world. A measured and powerful work'   *Irish Times*

'Edna O'Brien writes like the patron saint of sadness. Her Ireland is a place of heartbreak and betrayal where modern life co-exists painfully with ancient history ... Richly poetic'
Sunday Express

'So well written that you won't be disappointed whatever you are looking for. O'Brien rises like a lark in the clear air, she sings as she flies'   *Literary Review*

'O'Brien is a writer at the height of her powers'   *Tatler*

'O'Brien's prose is first-rate. She moves you to anger and fear and several other unspecified emotions simultaneously'
Literary Review

'The great Colette's mantle has fallen to Edna O'Brien – a darker writer, more full of conflict, O'Brien nonetheless shares the earthiness, the rawness, the chiselled prose, the scars of maturity. She is a consummate stylist and, to my mind, the most gifted woman now writing fiction in English'
Philip Roth

Edna O'Brien is the author of over twenty books, including *The Country Girls, Lantern Slides* (winner of the Premio Grinzane Cavour and the *Los Angeles Times* Prize) and *Time and Tide* (winner of the 1993 Writers' Guild Prize for Fiction) and a biography of James Joyce.

By the same author

The Country Girls
The Lonely Girl
Girls in their Married Bliss
August is a Wicked Month
Casualties of Peace
The Love Object and Other Stories
A Pagan Place
Zee & Co
Night
A Scandalous Woman and Other Stories
Mother Ireland
Johnny I Hardly Knew You
Mrs Reinhardt and Other Stories
Some Irish Loving – An Anthology
A Fanatic Heart
The High Road
Lantern Slides: Short Stories
Time and Tide
House of Splendid Isolation
Down by the River
Wild Decembers
James Joyce

Returning
Tales

EDNA O'BRIEN

PHOENIX

A Phoenix Paperback
First published in Great Britain by
George Weidenfeld & Nicolson in 1982
This paperback edition published in 1998
by Phoenix, a division of Orion Books Ltd,
Orion House, 5 Upper St Martin's Lane,
London WC2H 9EA

Reissued 2000

Grateful acknowledgement is made to the *New Yorker*,
in which several of the stories originally appeared.

A CIP catalogue record for this book
is available from the British Library.

ISBN: 0 75380 534 0

Printed and bound in Great Britain by
The Guernsey Press Co. Ltd.,
Guernsey, Channel Islands

In memory of Maureen Cusack

Contents

The Connor Girls

To know them would be to enter an exalted world. To open the stiff green iron gate, to go up their shaded avenue and to knock on their white hall door was a journey I yearned to make. No one went there except the gardener, the postman, and a cleaning woman who told none of their secrets, merely boasted that the oil paintings on the walls were priceless and the furniture was all antique. They had a flower garden with fountains, a water-lily pond, kitchen garden and ornamental trees that they called monkey-puzzle trees. Mr Connor, the Major, and his two daughters lived there. His only son had been killed in a car accident. It was said that the accident was due to his father's bullying of him, always urging him to drive faster since he had the most expensive car in the neighbourhood. Not even their tragedy brought them closer to the people in the town, partly because they were aloof, but being Protestants, the Catholics could not attend the service in the church or go to the Protestant graveyard where they had a vault with steps leading down to it, just like a house. It was smothered in creeper. They never went into mourning and had a party about a month later to which their friends came.

The Major had friends who owned a stud farm and these were invited two or three times a year along with a surgeon and his wife, from Dublin. The Connor girls were not beauties but they were distinguished and they talked in an accent that made everyone else's seem flat and sprawling, like some familiar estuary or a puddle in a field. They were dark haired with dark eyes and leathery skin. Miss Amy wore her hair in plaits which she folded over the crown of her head and Miss Lucy's hair, being more bushy, was kept flattened with brown slides. If they as much as nodded to a local or stopped to admire a new baby in its pram the news spread throughout the parish and those who had never had a salute felt such a pang of envy, felt left out. We ourselves had been saluted and it was certain that we would become on better terms since they were under a sort of compliment to us. My father had given them permission to walk their dogs over our fields so that most afternoons we saw the two girls in their white mackintoshes and biscuit-coloured walking sticks drawing these fawn unwieldy beasts, on leashes. Once they had passed our house they used to let their dogs go, whereupon our own sheep-dogs barked fiercely but kept inside our own paling being as I think terrified of the thorough-breds, who were beagles. Though they had been passing by for almost a year, they never stopped to talk to my mother if they met her returning from the hen-house with an empty pail, or going there with the foodstuff. They had merely saluted and passed on. They talked to my father of course and called him Mick, although his real name was Joseph, and they joked with him about his hunters which had never won cup or medal. They ignored my mother and she resented this. She longed to bring them in so that they could admire our house with all its knicknacks, and admire the thick wool rugs which she made in the winter nights and which she folded up when no visitors were expected.

'I'll ask them to tea this coming Friday,' she said to me. We planned to ask them impromptu, thinking that if we asked them ahead of time they were more likely to refuse. So we made cakes and sausage rolls and sandwiches of egg mayonnaise, some with onion, some without. The milk jelly we had made was whisked and seemed like a bowl of froth with a sweet confectionery smell. I was put on watch by the kitchen window and as soon as I saw them coming in at the gate I called to Mamma.

'They're coming, they're coming.'

She swept her hair back, pinned it with her brown tortoiseshell comb and went out and leaned on the top rung of the gate as if she was posing for a photograph, or looking at a view. I heard her say 'Excuse me Miss Connor, or rather Miss Connors,' in that exaggerated accent which she had picked up in America, and which she used when strangers came, or when she went to the city. It was like putting on new clothes or new shoes which did not fit her. I saw them shake their heads a couple of times and long before she had come back into the house I knew that the Connor girls had refused our invitation and that the table which we had laid with such ceremony was a taunt and a downright mockery.

Mamma came back humming to herself as if to pretend that it hadn't mattered a jot. The Connor girls had walked on and their dogs which were off the leashes were chasing our young turkeys into the woods.

'What will we do with this spread?' I asked Mamma as she put on her overall.

'Give it to the men, I expect,' she said wearily.

You may know how downcast she was when she was prepared to give iced cake and dainty sandwiches to workmen who were ploughing and whose appetites were ferocious.

'They didn't come,' I said stupidly, being curious to know how the Connor girls had worded their refusal.

'They never eat between meals,' Mamma said, quoting their exact phrase in an injured sarcastic voice.

'Maybe they'll come later on,' I said.

'They're as odd as two left shoes,' she said, tearing a frayed tea towel in half. When in a temper, she resorted to doing something about the house. Either she took the curtains down, or got on her knees to scrub the floor and the legs and rungs of the wooden chairs.

'They see no one except that Mad Man,' she said mainly to herself.

The Connor girls kept very much to themselves and did most of their shopping in the city. They attended church on Sundays, four Protestant souls comprising the congregation in a stone church that was the oldest in our parish. Moss covered the stones and various plants grew between the cracks so that in the

distance the side wall of the church was green both from ver-
dure and centuries of rain. Their father did not attend each
Sunday but once a month the girls wheeled him down to the
family vault where his wife and son were interred. Local people
who longed to be friends with them would rush out and offer
their sympathy as if the Major was the only one to have suffered
bereavement. Always he remained brusque and asked his
daughters the name of the man or woman who happened to be
talking to him. He was known to be crotchety but this was
because of his rheumatism which he had contracted years
before. He could not be persuaded to go to any of the holy wells
where other people went, to pray, and seek a cure for their
ailments. He was a large man with a very red face and he always
wore grey mittens. The Rector visited him twice a month and in
the dapping season sent up two fresh trout on the mail car. Soon
after the Connor girls invited the Rector for dinner and some of
the toffs who had come for the dapping.

Otherwise they entertained rarely, except for the Mad
Man who visited them every Sunday. He was a retired captain
from the next town and he had a brown moustache with a red
tint in it and very large bloodshot eyes. People said that he slept
with the Connor girls and hence he had been given the nickname of Stallion. It was him my mother referred to as the Mad
Man. On Sundays he drove over in his sports car, in time for
afternoon tea, which in summer time they had out of doors on
an iron table. Us children used to go over there to look at them
through the trees and though we could not clearly see them we
could hear their voices, hear the girls' laughter and then the tap
of a croquet mallet when they played a game. Their house was
approached from the road by a winding avenue that was dense
with evergreen trees. Those trees were hundreds of years old
but also there were younger trees that the Major had planted for
the important occasions in his life – the Coronation, the birth of
his children, England's victory in the last war. For his
daughters he had planted quinces. What were quinces we wondered and never found out. Nailed to the blue cedar, near the
gate was a sign which said 'Beware of dogs' and the white

pebble-dashed walls that surrounded their acres of garden were topped with broken glass so that children could not climb over and steal from the orchard.

Everyone vetted them when they came out of their stronghold on Sunday evening. Their escort, the Stallion, walked the girls to the Greyhound Hotel. Miss Amy, who was younger, wore brighter clothes but they both wore tweed costumes, and flat shoes with ornamental tongues that came over the insteps and hid the laces. Miss Amy favoured red or maroon while Miss Lucy wore dark brown with a matching dark-brown beret. In the hotel they had the exclusive use of the sitting room and sometimes when they were a little intoxicated Miss Lucy played the piano while her sister and the Stallion sang. It was a saucy song, a duet in which the man asked the pretty maid where she was going to, and eventually asked for her hand in marriage. Refusing him she said, 'I will not marry, marry, marry you', and then stamped her feet to emphasise it, whereupon the men in the bar would start laughing and saying Miss Amy was 'bucking'. There was much suggestiveness about their lives because the Stallion always spent Sunday night in their house. Hickey our hired help said they were all so drunk that they probably tumbled into bed together. Walking home on the frosty nights Hickey said it was a question of the blind leading the blind, as they slithered all over the road, and according to Hickey used language that was not ladylike. He would report these things in the morning to my mother and since they had rebuffed her she was pleased, and emphasised the fact that they had no breeding. Naturally she thought the very worst of the Stallion and could never bring herself to pronounce his christian name. To her he was 'that Mad Man'.

The Stallion was their sole escort until fate sent another man in the form of a temporary bank clerk. We reckoned that he was a Protestant because he didn't go to Mass on the first Sunday. He was most dashing. He had brown hair, he too had a moustache but it was fuller than the Stallion's and was a soft dark brown. Mostly he wore a tweed jacket and matching plus-fours. Also he had a motor cycle and when he rode it, he wore goggles. Within two weeks he was walking Miss Amy out and escorting her to the Greyhound Hotel. She began to pay more attention to her clothes, she got two new accordion-pleated skirts and some tight-fitting jumpers that made her bust more pronounced. They were called Sloppy Joe's but although they were long and sloppy they were also sleek, and they flattered the figure. Formerly her hair was wound in a staid plait around her head but now it was allowed to tumble down in thick coils over her shoulders and she toned down the colour in her cheeks with pale powder. No one ever said she was pretty but certainly she looked handsome when she cycled to the village to collect the morning paper, and hummed to herself as she went free-wheel down the hill that led to the town.

The bank clerk and herself were in love. Hickey saw them embrace in the porch of the Greyhound Hotel when Miss Lucy had gone back in to get a packet of cigarettes. Later they kissed shamelessly when walking along the towpath and people said that Miss Amy used to nibble the hairs of his luxurious mous-tache. One night she took off her sandal in the Greyhound Hotel and put her bare foot into the pocket of his sports jacket and the two of them giggled at her proceedings. Her sister and the Stallion often tagged along but Miss Amy and the bank clerk would set off on his motor cycle, down the Shannon Road, for fun. It was said that they swam naked but no one could verify that and it was possible that they just paddled their feet.

As it happened, someone brought mischievous news about the bank clerk. A commercial traveller who was familiar with other parts, told it on good authority that the bank clerk was a lapsed Catholic and had previously disgraced himself in a sea-side town. People were left to guess the nature of the mistake and most concluded that it concerned a girl or a woman. Instantly the parish turned against him. The next evening when he came out from the bank he found that both wheels of his pedal bicycle had been ripped and punctured and on the saddle there was an anonymous letter which read 'Go to Mass or we'll kill you.' His persecutors won. He attended the last Mass the following Sunday, knelt in the back pew with no beads and no prayer book, with only his fingers to pray on.

However it did not blight the romance. Those who had predicted that Miss Amy would ditch him because he was a Catholic were proven wrong. Most evenings they went down the Shannon Road, a couple full of glee, her hair and her headscarf flying, and chuckles of laughter from both of them as they frightened a dog or hens that strayed on to the roadside. Much later he saw her home, and the lights were on in their front parlour until all hours. A local person (the undertaker actually) thought of fitting up a telescope to try and see into the parlour but as soon as he went inside their front gate to reconnoitre, the dogs came rearing down the avenue and he ran for his life.

'Can it be serious I wonder.' So at last my mother admitted to knowing about the romance. She could not abide it, she said that Catholics and Protestants just could not mix. She recalled a grievance held for many years of a time in her girlhood when she and all the others from the national school were invited to the big house to a garden party, and were made to make fools of themselves by doing running jumps and sack races and were then given watery lemonade with flies in it. Her mind was firmly made up about the incompatibility of Catholics and Protestants. That very night Miss Amy sported an engagement ring in the Greyhound Hotel and the following morning the engagement was announced in the paper. The ring was star-shaped and comprised of tiny blue stones that sparkled and trembled under the beam of the hanging lamp. People gasped when told that it was insured for a hundred pounds.

'Do we have to give Miss Amy some sort of present,' my mother said grudgingly that evening. She had not forgotten how they snubbed her and how they barely thanked her for the fillets of pork that she gave them every time that we killed a pig.

'Indeed we do, and a good present,' my father said, so they went to Limerick some time after, and got a carving knife and fork that was packed in a velvet-lined box. We presented it to

Miss Amy the next time she was walking her dogs past our house.

'It *is* kind of you, thanks awfully,' she said as she smiled at each one of us, and told my father coyly that as she was soon to be hitched up they ought to have that night out. She was not serious of course but yet we all laughed and my mother did a 'tch tch' in mock disapproval. Miss Amy looked ravishing that day. Her skin was soft and her brown eyes had caught the reflection of her orange neck scarf and gave her a warm theatrical glow. Also she was amiable. It was a damp day, with shreds of mist on the mountains and the trees dripped quietly as we spoke. Miss Amy held out the palms of her hands to take the drips from the walnut tree and announced to the heavens what a 'lucky gal' she was. My mother enquired about her trousseau and was told that she had four pairs of court shoes, two camel-hair coats, a saxe-blue going-away suit and a bridal dress in voile that was a cross between peach and champagne colour. I loved her then, and wanted to know her and wished with all my heart that I could have gone across the fields with her and become her confidante but I was ten and she was thirty or thirty-five.

There was much speculation about the wedding. No one from the village had been invited but then that was to be expected. Some said that it was to be in a Register Office in Dublin but others said that the bank clerk had assured the Parish Priest that he would be married in a Catholic church, and had guaranteed a huge sum of money in order to get his letter of freedom. It was even said that Miss Amy was going to take instruction so as to be converted but that was only wishful thinking. People were stunned the day the bank clerk suddenly left. He left the bank at lunchtime, after a private talk with the Manager. Miss Amy drove him to the little railway station ten miles away, and they kissed several times before he jumped on to the moving train. The story was that he had gone ahead to make the plans and that the Connor girls and their father would travel shortly after. But the postman who was a Protestant said that the Major would not travel one inch to see his daughter marry a Papist.

We watched the house and gate carefully but we did not see Miss Amy emerge throughout the week. No one knows when she left, or what she wore or in what frame of mind. All we knew was that suddenly Miss Lucy was out walking with the Stallion and Miss Amy was not to be seen.

'And where's the bride-to-be tonight?' enquired Mrs O'Shea, the hotel proprietor. Miss Lucy's reply was clipped and haughty.

'My sister's gone away, for a change,' she said.

The frozen voice made everyone pause and Mrs O'Shea gave some sort of untoward gasp that seemed to detect catastrophe.

'Is there anything else you would care to know, Mrs O'Shea,' Miss Lucy asked and then turned on her heel and with the Stallion left. Never again did they drink in the Greyhound Hotel but moved to a public house up the street, where several of the locals soon followed them.

The mystery of Miss Amy was sending people into frenzies of conjecture and curiosity. Everyone thought that everyone else knew something. The postman was asked but he would just nod his head and say 'Time will tell', although it was plain to see that he was pleased with the outcome. The priest when asked in confidence by my mother said that the most Christian thing to do would be to go down on one's knees and say a prayer for Miss Amy. The phrase 'star-crossed lovers' was used by many of the women and for a while it even was suggested that Miss Amy had gone berserk and was shut up in an asylum. At last the suspense was ended as each wedding present was returned, with an obscure but polite note from Miss Lucy. My mother took ours back to the shop and got some dinner plates in exchange. The reason given was that there had been a clash of family interests. Miss Lucy came to the village scarcely at all. The Major had got more ill and she was busy nursing him. A night nurse cycled up their avenue every evening at five to nine, and the house itself, without so much coming and going, began to look forlorn. In the summer evenings I used to walk up the road and gaze in at it, admiring the green jalousies, the bird-table nailed to the tree, the tall important flowers and shrubs, that for want of tending had grown apace. I used to wish that I could unlock the gate and go up and be admitted there and find the clue to Miss Amy's whereabouts and her secret.

We did in fact visit the house the following winter when the Major died. It was much more simply furnished than I had imagined and the loose linen covers on the armchairs were a bit frayed. I was studying the portraits of glum puffy dark-looking ancestors when suddenly there was a hush and into the parlour came Miss Amy wearing a fur coat looking quite different. She looked older and her face was coarse.

'Miss Amy, Miss Amy,' several people said aloud, and flinching she turned to tell the driver to please leave her trunk on the landing upstairs. She had got much fatter and was wearing no engagement ring. When the people sympathised with her, her eyes became cloudy with tears and then she ran out of the room, and up the stairs to sit with the remains.

It did not take long for everyone to realise that Miss Amy had become a drinker. As the coffin was laid in the vault she tried to talk to her father which everyone knew was irrational. She did not just drink at night in the bar, but drank in the daytime and would take a miniature bottle out of her bag when she queued in the butcher's shop to get chops and a sheep's head for the dogs. She drank with my father when he was on a drinking bout. In fact she drank with anyone that would sit with her, and had lost all her snootiness. She sometimes referred to her engagement as 'My flutter'. Soon after, she was arrested in Limerick for drunken driving but was not charged because the Superintendent had been a close friend of her father's. Her driving became calamitous. People were afraid to let their children play in the street in case Miss Amy might run them over in her Peugeot car. No one had forgotten that her brother had killed himself driving and even her sister began to confide to my mother, telling her worries in tense whispers, spelling the words that were the most incriminating.

'It must be a broken heart,' my mother said.

'Of course with Dad gone there is no one to raise any objections now, to the wedding.'

'So why don't they marry,' my mother asked and in one fell swoop surrendered all her prejudices.

'Too late, too late,' Miss Lucy said and then added that Miss Amy could not get the bank clerk out of her system, that she sat in the breakfast room staring at photographs they had taken the day of her engagement and was always looking for an excuse to use his name.

One night the new Curate found Miss Amy drunk in a hedge under her bicycle. By then her driving licence had been taken away for a year. He picked her up, brought her home in his car and the next day called on her because he had found a brooch stuck to the fuchsia hedge where she became entangled. Furthermore he had put her bicycle in to be repaired. This gesture worked wonders. He was asked to stay to tea, and invited again the following Sunday. Due to his influence or perhaps secretly due to his prayers, Miss Amy began to drink less. To everyone's amazement the Curate went there most Sunday nights and played bridge with the two girls and the Stallion. In no time Miss Amy was overcome with resolve and industry. The garden which had been neglected began to look bright and trim again and she bought bulbs in the hardware shop, whereas formerly she used to send away to a nursery for them. Everyone remarked on how civil she had become. Herself and my mother exchanged recipes for apple jelly and lemon curd, and just before I went away to boarding school she gave me a present of a bound volume of Aesop's Fables. The print was so small that I could not read it, but it was the present that mattered. She handed it to me in the field and then asked if I would like to accompany her to gather some flowers. We went to the swamp to get the yellow irises. It was a close day, the air was thick with midges and they lay in hosts over the murky water. Holding a small bunch to her chest she said that she was going to post them to somebody, somebody special.

'Won't they wither,' I said, though what I really wanted to known was who they were meant for.

'Not if I pack them in damp moss,' she said and it seemed that the thought of despatching this little gift was bringing joy to her, though there was no telling who the recipient would be. She asked me if I'd fallen in love yet or had a 'beau'. I said that I had liked an actor who had come with the travelling players and had in fact got his autograph.

'Dreams', she said, 'dreams', and then using the flowers as a bat swatted some midges away. In September I went to boarding school and got involved with nuns and the various girl friends, and in time the people in our parish, even the Connor girls, almost disappeared from my memory. I never dreamt of them any more and I had no ambitions to go cycling with them or to visit their house. Later when I went to university in Dublin I learnt quite by chance that Miss Amy had worked in a beauty parlour in Stephens Green, had drank heavily, and had joined a golf club. By then the stories of how she teetered on high heels, or wore unmatching stockings or smiled idiotically and took ages to say what she intended to say, had no interest for me.

Somewhat precipitately and unknown to my parents I had become engaged to a man who was not of our religion. Defying threats of severing bonds, I married him and incurred the wrath of family and relatives just as Miss Amy had done, except that I was not there to bear the brunt of it. Horrible letters, some signed and some anonymous, used to reach me and my mother had penned an oath that we would never meet again, this side of the grave. I did not see my family for a few years, until long after my son was born, and having some change of heart they proposed by letter that my husband, my son and I, pay them a visit. We drove down one blowy autumn afternoon and I read stories aloud as much to distract myself as to pacify my son. I was quaking. The sky was watery and there were pale green patches like holes or voids in it. I shall never forget the sense of awkwardness, sadness and dismay when I stepped out of my husband's car and saw the large gaunt cut-stone house with thistles in the front garden. The thistle seed was blowing wildly, as were the leaves and even those that had already fallen were rising and scattering about. I introduced my husband to my parents and very proudly I asked my little son to shake hands with his grandfather, and his grandmother. They admired his gold hair but he ignored them and ran to cuddle the two sheepdogs. He was going to be the one that would make our visit bearable.

In the best room my mother had laid the table for tea and we sat and spoke to one another in thin, strained, unforgiving voices. The tea was too strong for my husband, who usually drank China tea anyhow, and instantly my mother jumped up to get some hot water. I followed her out to apologise for the inconvenience.

'The house looks lovely and clean,' I said.

She had polished everywhere and she had even dusted the artificial flowers which I remembered as being clogged with dust.

'You'll stay a month,' she said in a warm commandeering voice, and she put her arms around me in an embrace.

'We'll see,' I said prudently, knowing my husband's rest-lessness.

'You have a lot of friends to see,' she said.

'Not really,' I said with a coldness that I could not conceal.

'Do you know who is going to ask you to tea – the Connor girls.' Her voice was urgent and grateful. It meant a victory for her, for me, and an acknowledgement of my husband's non-religion. In her eyes Protestants and atheists were one and the same thing.

'How are they?' I asked.

'They've got very sensible, and aren't half as stuck up,' she said and then ran as my father was calling for her to cut the iced cake. Next afternoon there was a gymkhana over in the village and my parents insisted that we go.

'I don't want to go to this thing,' my husband said to me. He had intended to do some trout fishing in one of the many mountain rivers, and to pass his few days, as he said, without being assailed by barbarians.

'Just for this once,' I begged and I knew that he had consented because he put on his tie, but there was no affability in it. After lunch my father, my husband, my little son and I set out. My mother did not come as she had to guard her small chickens. She had told us in the most graphic details of her immense sorrow one morning upon finding sixty week-old chicks laid out on the flag dead, with their necks wrung, by weasels.

In the field where the gymkhana was held there were a few caravans, strains of accordion music, a gaudy sign announcing a Welsh clairvoyant, wild restless horses, and groups of self-conscious people in drab clothes, shivering as they waited for the events to begin. It was still windy and the horses looked unmanageable. They were being held in some sort of order by youngsters who had little power over them. I saw people stare in my direction and a few of them gave reluctant half-smiles. I felt uneasy and awkward and superior all at once.

'There's the Connor girls,' my father said. They were perched on their walking sticks which opened up to serve as little seats.

'Come on, come on,' he said excitedly and as we approached them they hailed me and said my name. They were older but still healthy and handsome, and Miss Amy showed no signs of her past despair. They shook my hand, shook my husband's hand and were quick to flirt with him, to show him what spirited girls they were.

'And what do you think of this young man,' my father said proudly as he presented his grandson.

'What a sweet little chap,' they said together, and I saw my husband wince. Then from the pocket of her fawn coat Miss Amy took two unwrapped jelly sweets and handed them to the little boy. He was on the point of eating them when my husband bent down until their faces were level and said very calmly, 'But you don't eat sweets, now give them back.' The little boy pouted, then blushed, and held out the palm of his hand on which rested these absurd two jellies that were dusted over with granular sugar. My father protested, the Connor girls let out exclamations of horror, and I said to my husband, 'Let him have them, it's a day out.' He gave me a menacing look and very firmly he repeated to the little boy what he had already said. The sweets were handed back and with scorn in her eyes Miss Amy looked at my husband and said, 'Hasn't the mummy got any say over her own child.'

There was a moment's strain, a moment's silence and then my father produced a packet of cigarettes and gave them one each. Since we didn't smoke we were totally out of things.

'No vices,' Miss Lucy said and my husband ignored her.

He suggested to me that we take the child across to where a man had a performing monkey clinging to a stick. He raised his cap slightly to say his farewell and I smiled as best I could. My father stayed behind with the Connor girls.

'They were going to ask us to tea,' I said to my husband as we walked downhill. I could hear the suction of his galoshes in the soggy ground.

'Don't think we missed much,' he said and at that moment I realised that by choosing his world I had said goodbye to my own and to those in it. By such choices we gradually become exiles, until at last we are quite alone.

My Mother's Mother

I loved my mother but yet I was glad when the time came to go to her mother's house each summer. It was a little house in the mountains and it commanded a fine view of the valley and the great lake below. From the front door, glimpsed through a pair of very old binoculars one could see the entire Shannon Lake studded with various islands. On a summer's day this was a thrill. I would be put standing on a kitchen chair, while someone held the binoculars and sometimes I marvelled though I could not see at all, as the lenses had not been focused properly. The sunshine made everything better and though we were not down by the lake, we imagined dipping our feet in it, or seeing people in boats fishing and then stopping to have a picnic. We imagined lake water lapping.

I felt safer in that house. It was different to our house, not so imposing, a cottage really, with no indoor water or no water closet. We went for buckets of water to the well, a different well each summer. These were a source of miracle to me, these deep cold wells, sunk into the ground, in a kitchen garden, or a paddock or even a long distance away, wells that had been divined since I was last there. There was always a tin scoop nearby so that one could fill the bucket to the very brim. Then of course the full bucket was an occasion of trepidation because one was supposed not to spill. One often brought the bucket to the very threshold of the kitchen and then out of excitement or clumsiness some would get splashed on to the concrete floor and there would be admonishments but it was not like the admonishments in our own house, it was not calamitous.

My grandfather was old and thin and hoary when I first

saw him. His skin was the colour of a clay pipe. After the market days he would come home in the pony and trap drunk, and then as soon as he stepped out of the trap he would stagger and fall into a drain or whatever. Then he would roar for help and his grandson, who was in his twenties, would pick him up, or rather drag him along the ground and through the house, and up the stairs to his feather bed where he moaned and groaned. The bedroom was above the kitchen and in the night we would be below, around the fire eating warm soda bread, and drinking cocoa. There was nothing like it. The fresh bread would only be an hour out of the pot, and cut in thick pieces and dolloped with butter and greengage jam. The greengage jam was a present from the postmistress who gave it in return for the grazing of a bullock. She gave marmalade at a different time of year and a barm-brack at Halloween. He moaned upstairs but no one was frightened of him, not even his own wife who chewed and chewed and said, 'Bad cess to them that give him the drink.' She meant the publicans. She was a minute woman with a minute face and her thin hair was pinned up tightly. Her little face, though old, was like a bud and when she was young she had been beautiful. There was a photo of her to prove it.

Sitting with them at night I thought that maybe I would not go home at all. Maybe I would never again lie in bed next to my mother, the two of us shivering with expectancy and with terror. Maybe I would forsake my mother.

'Maybe you'll stay here,' my aunt said, as if she had guessed my thoughts.

'I couldn't do that,' I said, not knowing why I declined because indeed the place had definite advantages. I stayed up as late as they did. I ate soda bread and jam to my heart's content, I rambled around the fields all day, admiring sally trees, elder bushes and the fluttering flowers, I played 'shop' or I played teaching in the little dark plantation, and no one interfered or told me to stop doing it. The plantation was where I played secrets and always I knew the grown-ups were within shouting distance, if a stranger or a tinker should surprise me there. It was pitch dark and full of young fir trees. The ground was a carpet of bronzed fallen fir needles. I used to kneel on them for punishment, after the playing.

Then when that ritual was done I went into the flower garden, which being full of begonias and lupins was a mass of bright brilliant colours. Each area had its own colour as my aunt planned it that way. I can see them now, those bright reds, like nail varnish, and those yellows like the gauze of a summer dress and those pale blues like old people's eyes, with the bees and the wasps luxuriating in each petal, or each little bell, or each flute, and the warmth of the place, and the drone of the bees, and my eyes lighting on tea towels, and flannel drawers and the various things spread out on the hedge to dry. The sun garden they called it. My aunt got the seeds and just sprinkled them around causing marvellous blooms to spring up. They even had tulips whereas at home we had only a diseased rambling rose on a silvered arch and two clumps of devil's pokers. Our garden was sad and windy, the wind had made holes and indentations in the hedges, and the dogs had made further holes where they slept and burrowed. Our house was larger, and there was better linoleum on the floor, there were brass rods on the stairs, and there was a flush lavatory but it did not have the same cheeriness and it was imbued with doom.

Still I knew that I would not stay in my grandmother's forever. I knew it for certain when I got into bed and then desperately missed my mother, and missed the little whispering we did, and the chocolate we ate, and I missed the smell of our kind of bedclothes. Theirs were grey flannel that tickled the skin, as did the loose feathers and their pointed ends kept irking one. There was a gaudy red quilt that I thought would come to life, and turn into a sinister Santa Claus. Except that they had told me that there was no Santa Claus. My aunt told me that, she insisted.

There was my aunt and her two sons Donal and Joe, and my grandmother and grandfather. Donal had gone away to England to be near a girl. My aunt and Joe would tease me each night, say that there was no Santa Claus, until I got up and stamped the floor and in contradicting them welled up with tears, and then at last when on the point of breaking down they would say that there was. Then one night they went too far. They said that my mother was not my real mother. My real mother, they said, was in Australia and that I was adopted. I could not be told that word. I began to hit the wall, and screech and the more they insisted the more obstreperous I became. My aunt went into the parlour in search of a box of snaps to find a photo of my real mother and came out triumphant, at having found it. She showed me a woman in knickerbockers with a big floppy hat. I could have thrown it in the fire so violent was I. They watched for each new moment of panic, and furious disbelief, and then they got the wind up when they saw I was getting out of control. I began to shake like the weather conductor on the chapel chimney and my teeth chattered, and before long I was just this shaking creature, unable to let out any sound and, seeing the room's contents swim away from me, I felt their alarm almost as I felt my own. My aunt took hold of my wrist to feel my pulse, and my grandmother held a spoonful of tonic to my lips but I spilt it. It was called Parishes Food and was the colour of cooked beetroot. My eyes were haywire. My aunt put a big towel around me, and sat me on her knee, and as the terror lessened my tears began to flow and I cried so much that they thought I would choke because of the tears going back down the throat. They said I must never tell anyone and I must never tell my mother.

'She is my mother,' I said, and they said, 'Yes darling', but I knew that they were appalled at what had happened.

That night, I fell out of bed twice and my aunt had to put chairs to it to keep me in. She slept in the same room and often I used to hear her crying for her dead husband and begging to be reunited with him in heaven. She used to talk to him and say, 'Is that you Michael, is that you?' I often heard her arms striking against the head-board, or her heavy movements when she got up to relieve herself. In the daytime we used the fields but at night we did not go out for fear of ghosts. There was a gutter in the back kitchen that served as a channel and twice a week she put disinfectant in it. The crux in the daytime was finding a private place and not being found or spied on by anyone. It entailed much walking and then much hesitating so as not to be seen.

The morning after the fright, they pampered me, scrambled me an egg and sprinkled nutmeg over it. Then along with that my aunt announced a surprise. Our workman had sent word by the mail-car man that he was coming to see me on the Sunday and the postman had delivered the message. Oh what a glut of happiness. Our workman was called 'Carnero' and I loved him too. I loved his rotting teeth, and his curly hair, and his strong hands, and his big stomach that people referred to as his 'corporation'. He was nicknamed Carnero after a boxer. I knew that when he came he would have bars of chocolate, and maybe a letter or a silk hanky from my mother, and that he would lift me up in his arms and swing me around and say 'Sugarbush'. How many hours were there until Sunday, I asked.

Yet that day, which was a Friday, did not pass without event. We had a visitor – a man. I will never know why but my grandfather called him Tim, whereas his real name was Pat, but my grandfather was not to be told that. Tim it seems, had died and my grandfather was not to know because if any of the locals died, it brought his own death to his mind and he dreaded death as strenuously as did all the others. Death was some weird journey that you made alone, and unbefriended, once you had embarked on it. When my aunt's husband had died, in fact had been shot by the Black and Tans, my aunt had to conceal the death from her own parents so irrational were they about the subject. She had to stay up at home the evening her husband's remains were brought to the chapel and when the chapel bell rang out intermittently, as it does for a death, and they asked who it was, again and again, my poor aunt had to conceal her own grief, be silent about her own tragedy, and pretend that she did not know. Next day she went to the funeral on the excuse that it was some forester whom her husband knew. Her husband was supposed to be transferred to a barracks a long way off, and meanwhile she was going to live with her parents and bring her infant sons until her husband found accommodation. She invented a name for the district where her husband was supposed to be, it was in the north of Ireland, and she invented letters that she had received from him, and the news of the 'Troubles' up there. Eventually I expect she told them, and I expect they collapsed and broke down. In fact the man who brought these imaginary letters would have been Tim, since he had been the postman, and it was of his death my grandfather must not be told. So there in the porch, in a worn suit, was a man called Pat answering to the name of Tim, and the news that a Tim would have, such as how were his family, and what crops had he put in, and what cattle fairs had he been to. I thought that it was peculiar that he could answer for another but I expect that everyone's life story was identical.

Sunday after Mass I was down by the little green gate skipping and waiting for Carnero. As often happens the visitor arrives just when we look away. The cuckoo called, and though I knew I would not see her I looked in a tree where there was a ravaged bird's nest, and at that moment heard Carnero's whistle. I ran down the road and at once he hefted me up onto the crossbar of his bicycle.

'Oh Carnero,' I cried. There was both joy and sadness in our reunion. He had brought me a bag of tinned sweets, and the most glamorous present – and as we got off the bicycle near the little gate he put it on me. It was a toy watch – a most beautiful red and each bit of the bracelet was the shape and colour of a raspberry. It had hands and though they did not move that did not matter. One could pull the bracelet part by its elastic thread and cause it to snap in or out. The hands were black and frail like an eyelash. He would not say where he had got it. I had only one craving, to stay down there by the gate with him and admire the watch and talk about home. I could not talk to him in front of them because a child was not supposed to talk or have any wants. He was puffing from having cycled uphill and began to open his tie and taking it off he said, 'This bloody thing.' I wondered who he had put it on for. He was in his Sunday suit and had a fishing feather in his hat.

'Oh Carnero, turn the bike around and bring me home with you.'

Such were my unuttered and unutterable hopes. Later my grandfather teased me and said was it in his backside I saw Carnero's looks and I said no, in every particle of him.

That night as we were saying the Rosary my grandfather let out a shout, slouched forward, knocking the wooden chair and hitting himself on the rungs of it, then falling on the cement floor. He died delirious. He died calling on his Maker. It was ghastly. Joe was out and only my grandmother and aunt were there to assist. They picked him up. His skin was purple, and the exact colour of the iron tonic, and his eyes rolled so that they were seeing every bit of the room, from the ceiling, to the whitewashed wall, to the cement floor to the settle bed, to the cans of milk, seeing and bulging. He writhed like an animal and then let out a most beseeching howl and that was it. At that moment my aunt remembered I was there, and told me to go into the parlour and wait. It was worse in there, pitch dark and I in a place where I did not know my footing, or my way around. I'd only been in there once to fetch a teapot and a sugar tongs when Tim came. Had it been in our own house I would have known what to cling to, the back of a chair, the tassel of a blind, the girth of a plaster statue, but in there I held on to nothing and thought how the thing he dreaded had come to pass and now he was finding out those dire things that all his life his mind had barely kept at bay.

'May he rest in peace, may the souls of the faithful departed rest in peace.'

It was that for two days, along with litanies, and mourners smoking clay pipes, plates of cake being passed around and glasses filled. My mother and father were there, among the mourners. I was praised for growing, as if it was something I myself had caused to happen. My mother looked older in black, and I wished she had worn a georgette scarf, something to give her a bit of brightness around the throat. She did not like when I said that, and sent me off to say the Confiteor and three Hail Marys. Her eyes were dry. She did not love her own father. Neither did I. Her sister and she would go down into the far room, and discuss whether to bring out another bottle of whiskey or another porter cake or whether it was time to offer the jelly. They were reluctant. The reason being that some provisions had to be held over for the next day, when the special mourners would come up after the funeral. Whereas that night half the parish was there. My grandfather was laid out upstairs in a brown habit. He had stubble on his chin and looked like a frosted plank lying there, grey-white and inanimate. As soon as they had paid their respects, the people hurried down to the kitchen, and the parlour, for the eats and the chat. No one wanted to be with the dead man, not even his wife, who had gone a bit funny and was asking my aunt annoying questions about the food and the fire, and how many priests were going to serve at the High Mass.

'Leave that to us,' my mother would say, and then my grandmother would re-tell the world what a palace my mother's house was, and how it was the nicest house in the countryside and my mother would say 'Shhhh', as if she was being disgraced. My father said, 'Well Missy' to me twice, and a strange man gave me sixpence. It was a very thin worn sixpence and I thought it would disappear. I called him Father, out of reverence because he looked like a priest but he was in fact a boatman.

The funeral was to an island on the Shannon. Most of the people stayed on the quay, but we, the family, piled into two rowboats and followed the boat that carried the coffin. It was a jolty ride with big waves coming in over us and our feet getting drenched. The island itself was full of cows. The sudden arrivals made them bawl and race about, and I thought it was quite improper to see that happening, while the remains were being lowered and buried. It was totally desolate, and though my aunt sniffled a bit, and my grandmother let out ejaculations, there was no real grief and that was the saddest thing.

Next day they burned his working clothes and threw his muddy boots on to the manure heap. Then my aunt sewed black diamonds of cloth on her clothes, on my grandmother's and on Joe's. She wrote a long letter to her son in England, and enclosed black diamonds of cloth for him to stitch on to his effects. He worked in Liverpool in a motor car factory. Whenever they said Liverpool I thought of a whole mound of bloodied liver, but then I would look down at my watch and be happy again and pretend to tell the time. The house was gloomy. I went off with Joe who was mowing hay and sat with him on the mowing machine and fell slightly in love. Indoors was worst, what with my grandmother sighing, and recalling old times, such as when her husband tried to kill her with a carving knife, and then she would snivel and miss him and say 'The poor old creature, he wasn't prepared . . .'

Out in the fields Joe fondled my knee and asked was I ticklish. He had a lovely long face and a beautiful whistle. He was probably about twenty-four, but he seemed old, especially because of a slouchy hat and because of a pair of trousers that were several times too big for him. When the mare passed water he nudged me and said 'Want lemonade?' and when she broke wind he made disgraceful plopping sounds with his lips. He and I ate lunch on the headland and lolled for a bit. We had bread and butter, milk from a flask, and some ginger cake that was left over since the funeral. It had gone damp. He sang 'You'll be lonely little sweetheart in the Spring', and smiled a lot at me and I felt very important. I knew that all he would do was tickle my knees, and the backs of my knees, because at heart he was shy, and not like some of the local men who would want to throw you to the ground, and press themselves over you so that you would have to ask God for protection. When he lifted me on to the machine he said that we would bring out a nice little cushion on the morrow so that I would have a soft seat. But on the morrow it rained and he went off to the sawmill to get shelving, and my aunt moaned about the hay getting wet and perhaps getting ruined and possibly there being no fodder for cattle next winter.

That day I got into dire disaster. I was out in the fields playing, talking, and enjoying the rainbows in the puddles, when all of a sudden I decided to run helter-skelter towards the house in case they were cross with me. Coming through a stile that led to the yard I decided to do a big jump and landed head over heels into the manure heap. I fell so heavily on to it that every bit of clothing got wet and smeared. It was a very massive manure heap, and very squelchy. Each day the cow house was cleaned out and the contents shovelled there, and each week the straw and old nesting from the hen-house was dumped there, and so was the pigs' bedding. So it was not like falling into a sack of hay. It was not dry and clean. It was a foul spot I fell into, and as soon as I got my bearings I decided it was wise to undress. The pleated skirt was ruined and so was my blouse and my navy cardigan. Damp had gone through to my bodice and the smell was dreadful. I was trying to wash it off under an outside tap, using a fist of grass as a cloth, when my aunt came out and exclaimed, 'Jesus, Mary and Joseph, glory be to the great God today and tonight but what have you done to yourself!' I was afraid to tell her that I fell, so I said I was doing washing and she said in the name of God what washing, and then she saw the ruin on the garments. She picked up the skirt and said why on earth had she let me wear it that day, and wasn't it the demon that came with me the day I arrived with my attaché case. I was still trying to wash and not answer this barrage of questions, all beginning with the word 'why'. As if I knew why! She got a rag and some pumice stone, plus a can of water, and, stripped to the skin, I was washed and reprimanded. Then my clothes were put to soak in the can, all except for the skirt which had to be brought in to dry, and then cleaned with a clothes-brush. Mercifully my grandmother was not told.

My aunt forgave me two nights later when she was in the dairy churning, and singing. I asked if I could turn the churn handle for a jiff. It was changing from liquid to solid and the handle was becoming stiff. I tried with all my might but I was not strong enough.

'You will, when you're big,' she said and sang to me. She sang 'Far Away in Australia' and then asked what I would like to do when I grew up. I said I would like to marry Carnero and she laughed and said what a lovely thing it was to be young and carefree. She let me look into the churn to see the mound of yellow butter that had formed. There were drops of water all over its surface, it was like some big bulk that had bathed, but had not dried off. She got two sets of wooden pats and together we began to fashion the butter into dainty shapes. She was quicker at it than I. She made little round balls of butter with prickly surfaces, then she said wouldn't it be lovely if the Curate came up for tea. He was a new Curate and had rimless spectacles.

The next day she went to the town to sell the butter and I was left to mind the house along with my grandmother. My aunt had promised to bring back a shop cake, and said that depending on the price it would either be a sponge cake or an Oxford Lunch which was a type of fruit cake wrapped in beautiful shiny silver paper. My grandmother donned a big straw hat, with a chin strap, and looked very distracted. She kept thinking that there was a car or a cart coming into the back yard and had me looking out windows on the alert. Then she got a flush and I had to conduct her into the plantation, and sit on the bench next to her, and we were scarcely there, when three huge fellows walked in, and we knew at once that they were tinkers. The fear is indescribable. I knew that tinkers took one off in their cart, hid one under shawls, and did dire things to one. I knew that they beat their wives and children, got drunk, had fights amongst themselves and spent many a night cooling off in the barracks. I jumped up as they came through the gate. My grandmother's mouth fell wide open with shock. One of them carried a shears and the other had a weighing pan in his hand. They asked if we had any sheep's wool and we both said no, no sheep, only cattle. They had evil eyes and gamey looks. There was no knowing what they would do to us. Then they asked if we had any feathers for pillows or mattresses. She was so crazed with fear that she said yes and led the way to the house. As we walked along I expected a strong hand to be clamped on my shoulder. They were dreadfully silent. Only one had spoken and he had a shocking accent, what my mother would call 'a gurrier's'. She sent me upstairs to get the two bags of feathers, out of the wardrobe, and I knew that she stayed below so that they would not steal a cake of bread, or crockery or any other thing. She was agreeing a price when I came down or rather requesting a price. The talking member said it was a barter job. We would get a lace cloth in return. She asked how big this cloth was, and he said very big, while his companion put his hand into the bag of feathers, to make sure that there was not anything else in there, that we were not trying to fob them off with grass or sawdust or something. She asked where was the cloth. They laughed. They said it was down in the caravan, at the cross-roads, ma'am. She knew then she was being cheated, but she tried to stand her ground. She grabbed one end of the bag and said 'You'll not have these.'

'D'you think we're mugs,' one of them said, and gestured to the others to pick up the two bags, which they did. Then they looked at us as if they might mutilate us and I prayed to St Jude and St Anthony to keep us from harm. Before going, they insisted on being given new milk. They drank in great slugs.

'Are you afraid of me?' one of the men said to her.

He was the tallest of the three and his shirt was open. I could see the hair on his chest and he had a very funny look in his eyes like as if he was not thinking, like as if thinking was beyond him. His eyes had a thickness in them. For some reason he reminded me of meat.

'Why should I be afraid of you,' she said and I was so proud of her I would have clapped, but for the tight shave we were in.

She blessed herself several times when they'd gone and decided, that what we did, had been the practical thing to do, and in fact our only recourse. But when my aunt came back and began an intensive cross-examination the main contention was how they learnt in the first place that there were feathers in the house. My aunt reasoned that they could not have known unless they had been told, they were not fortune-tellers. Each time I was asked, I would seal my lips as I did not want to betray my grandmother. Each time she was asked, she described them in detail, the holes in their clothes, the safety pins instead of buttons, their villainous looks, and then she mentioned the child, me, and hinted about the things they might have done and was it not the blessing of God that we had got rid of them peaceably! My aunt's son joked about the lace cloth for weeks. He used to affect to admire it, by picking up one end of the black oilcloth on the table and saying, 'Is it Brussels lace or is it Carrickmackross?'

Sunday came and my mother was expected to visit. My aunt had washed me the night before in an aluminium pan. I had to sit into it, and was terrified lest my cousin should peep in. He was in the back kitchen shaving and whistling. It was a question of a 'Saturday splash for Sunday's dash'. My aunt poured a can of water over my head and down my back. It was scalding hot. Then she poured rainwater over me and by contrast it was freezing. She was not a thorough washer like my mother but all the time she kept saying that I would be like a new pin.

My mother was not expected until the afternoon. We had washed up the dinner things and given the dogs the potato skins and milk when I started in earnest to look out for her. I went to the gate where I had waited for Carnero and seeing no sign of her I sauntered off down the road. I was at the crossroads when I realised how dangerous it was, as I was approaching the spot where the tinkers said their caravan was pitched. So it was back at full speed. The fuchsia was out and so were the elderberries. The fuchsia was like dangling earrings and the riper elderberries were in maroon smudges on the road. I waited in hiding the better to surprise her. She never came. It was five, and then half past five, and then it was six. I would go back to the kitchen and lift the clock that was face down on the dresser, and then hurry out to my watch post. By seven it was certain that she would not come although I still held out hope. They hated to see me sniffle and even hated more when I refused a slice of cake. I could not bear to eat. Might she still come? They said there was no point in my being so spoilt. I was imprisoned at the kitchen table in front of this slice of seed cake. In my mind I lifted the gate hasp a thousand times, and saw my mother pass by the kitchen window, as fleeting as a ghost, and by the time we all knelt down to say the Rosary my imagination had run amuck. I conceived of the worst things, such as she had died, or that my father had killed her or that she had met a man and eloped. All three were unbearable. In bed I sobbed and chewed on the blanket so as not to be heard, and between tears and with my aunt enjoining me to dry up, I hatched a plan.

On the morrow there was no word or no letter so I decided to run away. I packed a little satchel with bread, my comb, and daftly a spare pair of ankle socks. I told my aunt that I was going on a picnic and affected to be very happy by humming and doing little reels. It was a dry day and the dust rose in whirls under my feet. The dogs followed and I had immense trouble getting them to go back. There were no tinkers' caravans at the crossroads and because of that I was jubilant. I walked and then ran, and then I would have to slow down and always when I slowed down I looked back in case someone was following me. While I was running I felt I could elude them but there was no eluding the loose stones, and the bits of rock that were wedged into the dirt road. Twice I tripped. If, coming towards me, I saw two people together I then felt safe but if I saw one person it boded ill, as that one person could be mad, or drunk, or ready to accost. On three occasions I had to climb into a field and hide until that one ominous person went by. Fortunately it was a quiet road as not many souls lived in that region.

When I came off the dirt road onto the main road I felt safer and very soon a man came by in a pony and trap and offered me a lift. He looked a harmless enough person, in a frieze coat and a cloth cap. When I stepped into the trap I was surprised to find two hens clucking and agitating under a seat.

'Would you be one of the Linihans?' he asked, referring to my grandmother's family.

I said no and gave an assumed name. He plied me with questions. To get the most out of me he even got the pony to slow down, so as to lengthen the journey. We dawdled. The seat of black leather was held down with black buttons. He had a tartan rug over him. He spread it out over us both. Quickly I edged out from under it complaining about fleas and midges, neither of which there were. It was a desperately lonely road with only a house here and there, a graveyard, and sometimes an orchard. The apples looked tempting on the trees. To see each ripening apple was to see a miracle. He asked if I believed in ghosts and told me that he had seen the riderless horse, on the moors.

'If you're a Minnogue,' he said, 'you should be getting out here', and he pulled on the reins.

I had called myself a Minnogue because I knew a girl of that name who lived with her mother and was separated from her father. I would like to have been her.

'I'm not,' I said, and tried to be as innocent as possible. I then had to say who I was, and ask if he would drop me in the village.

'I'm passing your gate,' he said, and I was terrified that I would have to ask him up as my mother dreaded strangers, even dreaded visitors, since these diversions usually gave my father the inclination to drink and once he drank he was on a drinking bout that would last for weeks and that was notorious. Therefore I had to conjure up another lie. It was that my parents were both staying with my grandmother and that I had been despatched home to get a change of clothing for us all. He grumbled at not coming up to our house but I jumped out of the trap and said we would ask him to a card party for sure, in December.

There was no one at home. The door was locked and the big key in its customary place under the pantry window. The kitchen bore signs of my mother having gone out in a hurry as the dishes were on the table, and on the table too was her powder puff, a near-empty powder box, and a holder of papier mâché in which her toiletries were kept. Had she gone to the city? My heart was wild with envy. Why had she gone without me? I called upstairs and then hearing no reply I went up with a mind that was buzzing with fear, rage, suspicion and envy. The beds were made. The rooms seemed vast and awesome compared with the little crammed rooms of my grandmother's. I heard someone in the kitchen and hurried down with renewed palpitations. It was my mother. She had been to the shop and got some chocolate. It was rationed because of its being wartime, but she used to coax the shopkeeper to give her some. He was a bachelor. He liked her. Maybe that was why she had put powder on.

'Who brought you home, my lady?' she said stiffly.

She hadn't come on Sunday. I blurted that out. She said did anyone ever hear such nonsense. She said did I not know that I was to stay there until the end of August till school began. She was even more irate when she heard that I had run away. What would they now be thinking, but that I was in a bog home or something. She said had I no consideration and how in heaven's name was she going to get word to them, an sos.

'Where's my father?' I asked.

'Saving hay,' she said.

I gathered the cups off the table so as to make myself useful in her eyes. Seeing the state of my canvas shoes, and the marks on the ankle socks she asked had I come through a river or what. All I wanted to know was why she had not come on Sunday as promised. The bicycle got punctured she said and then asked did I think that with bunions, corns and welts she could walk six miles after doing a day's work. All I thought was that the homecoming was not nearly as tender as I hoped it would be, and there was no embrace and no reunion. She filled the kettle and I laid clean cups. I tried to be civil, to contain the pique and the misery that was welling up in me. I told her how many trams of hay they had made in her mother's house and she said it was a sight more than we had done. She hauled some scones from a colander in the cupboard and told me I had better eat. She did not heat them on the top of the oven and that meant she was still vexed. I knew that before nightfall she would melt, but where is the use of a thing that comes too late.

I sat at the far end of the table watching the lines on her brow, watching the puckering, as she wrote a letter to my aunt explaining that I had come home. I would have to give it to the mail-car man the following morning and ask the postman to deliver it by hand. She said God only knows what commotion there would be all that day and into the night looking for me. The ink in her pen gave out and I held the near-empty ink bottle sideways while she refilled it.

'Go back to your place,' she said and I went back to the far end of the table like someone glued to her post. I thought of the fields around my grandmother's house and the various smooth stones that I had put on the windowsill, I thought of the sun garden, of the night my grandfather had died and my vigil in the cold parlour. I thought of many things. Sitting there I both wanted to be in our house and to be back in my grandmother's missing my mother. It was as if I could taste my pain better away from her, the excruciating pain that told me how much I loved her. I thought how much I needed to be without her so that I could think of her, dwell on her, and fashion her into the perfect person that she clearly was not. I resolved that for certain I would grow up and one day go away. It was a sweet thought and it was packed with punishment.

Tough Men

'Throw more paraffin in it,' Morgan said as he went out to the shop to serve Mrs Gleeson for the sixth time that morning. Hickey threw paraffin and a fist of matches onto the grey cinders, then put the top back on the stove quickly in case the flames would leap into his face. The skewers of curled-up bills on the shelf overhead were scorched, having almost caught fire many a time before. It was a small office partitioned off from the shop, where Morgan did his accounts and kept himself warm in the winter. A cosy place with two chairs, a sloping wooden desk, and ledgers going back so far that most of the names entered in the early ones were the names of dead people. There was a safe as well and everything had the air of being undisturbed because the ashes and dust had congealed evenly on things. It was called The Snug.

'Bloody nuisance that Gleeson woman,' Morgan said as he came in from the counter and touched the top of the iron stove to see if it was warming up.

'She doesn't do a tap of work; hubby over in England earning money, all the young ones out stealing firewood, and milk, and anything else they can lay hands on,' Hickey said.

Mrs Gleeson was an inquisitive woman, always dressed in black with a black kerchief over her head and a white, miserable, nosey face.

'We'll need to get a good fire up,' Morgan said. 'That's one thing we'll need', and he popped a new candle into the stove to get it going. He swore by candlegrease and paraffin for lighting fires, and neither cost him anything because he sold them, along with every other commodity that country people needed – tea, flour, henfood, hardware, wellington boots and gaberdine coats. In the summer he hung the coats outside the door, on a window ledge and once a coat had fallen into a puddle. He offered it to Hickey cheap, but was rejected.

'Will they miss you?' Morgan said.

'Miss my eye! Isn't poor man in bed with hot water bottles and Sloans liniment all over Christmas, and she's so murdered minding him, she doesn't know what time of day it is.'

'Poor man,' was Hickey's name for his boss Mr James Brady, a gentleman farmer who was given to drink, rheumatic aches and a ferocious temper.

'Say the separating machine got banjaxed up at the creamery,' Morgan said.

'Of course,' said Hickey as if any fool would know enough to say that. It was simple; Hickey had been to the creamery with Brady's milk, and when he got home he could say he had been held up because a machine broke down.

'Of course I'll tell them that,' he said again and winked at Morgan. They were having an important caller that morning and a lot of strategy was required. Morgan opened the lower flap door of the stove and a clutter of ashes fell onto his boots. The grating was choked with ashes too and Hickey began to clean it out with a stick so that they could at least make the place presentable. Then he rooted in the turf basket and finding two logs he popped them in, and emptied whatever shavings and turf dust were in the basket over them.

'That stove must be thirty years old,' Morgan said, remembering how he used to light it with balls of paper and dry sticks when he first came to work in the shop as an apprentice. He lit it all the years he served his time and he still lit it when he began to get wise to fiddling money and giving short weight. That was when he was saving to buy the shop from the mean blackguard who owned it. He even lit it when he hired the new shop-girl because she was useless at it. She had chilblains and hence wore a dress down to her ankles, and he pitied her for her foolishness. Finally he married her. Now he had a shop-boy who usually lit the stove for him.

'His nibs is off again today,' he said to Hickey, remembering the squint-eyed shop-boy whom he hired but did not trust.

'He'd stay at home with a gumboil, he would,' Hickey said, though neither of them objected very much as they needed the privacy. Also business was being slack just after Christmas.

'If this thing comes off we'll go to the dogs, Fridays and Saturdays,' Morgan said.

'Shanks mare?' Hickey asked with a grin.

'We'll hire a car,' Morgan said and the dreams of these pleasant outings began to buoy him up and make him smile in anticipation. He liked the dogs and already envisaged the crowds, the excitement, the tote board, the tracks artificially lit up and the six or seven sleek hounds following the hare with such grace as if it was wind and not their own legs that propelled them.

'Let's do our sums,' he said and together Hickey and himself counted the number of big farmers who had hay-sheds. Not having been up the country for many a day Morgan was, as he admitted, hazy about who lived beyond the chapel road, or up the commons, or down the Coolnahilla way and in the by-roads and over the hills. In this Hickey was fluent because he did a bit of shooting on Sundays and had walked those Godforsaken spots. They counted the farmers and hence the number of hay-sheds and their eyes shone with cupidity and glee. The stranger who was coming to see them had patented a marvellous stuff, that when sprayed on hay-sheds prevented rusting. Morgan was hoping to be given the franchise for the whole damn parish.

'Jaysus, there must be a hundred hay-sheds,' Hickey said, and marvelled at Morgan's good luck at meeting a man who put him on to such a windfall.

' 'Twas pure fluke,' Morgan said and recalled the holiday he took at the spa town and how one day when he was trying to down this horrible sulphur water a man sat next to him and asked him where he was from, and eventually he heard about this substance that was a godsend to farmers.

'Pure fluke,' he said again and lifted the whiskey bottle

from its hiding place, behind a holy picture which was laid against the wall. He took a quick slug.

'I think that's him,' Hickey said, buttoning his waistcoat so as not to seem like a barbarian. In fact it was John Ryan, a medical student, who had been asked not for reasons of his education but because he had a bit of pull. He tiptoed towards the entrance and from the outside played on the frosted glass as if it were a piano.

'Come in,' said Morgan.

He knew it was John Ryan by the shape of the long eejitty fingers. Ryan was briefed to tell them if any other shopkeepers up the street had been approached by the bloke. Being home on holidays, Ryan did nothing but hatch in houses, drink tea, and click girls in the evening.

'All set,' said Ryan as he looked at the two men and the saucepan waiting on the stove. Morgan had decided that they would do a bit of cooking, having reasoned that if a man came all that way a bit of grub would not go amiss. Hickey who couldn't even go to the creamery without bringing a large agricultural sandwich in his pocket, declared that no man does good business on an empty stomach. The man was from the North of Ireland.

'Is the bird on yet?' said John Ryan, splaying his hands fanwise to get a bit of heat from the stove.

'We haven't got her yet,' said Hickey and Morgan cursed aloud the farmer that had promised him a cockerel.

'Get us a few logs while you're standing,' Morgan said and John Ryan reluctantly went out. At the back of the shop by a mossy wall he gathered a bundle of damp roughly sawn logs. He was in dread that he would stain the new fawn Crombie coat that his mother had given him at Christmas.

'Any sign of anyone?' Morgan said. It was important that the man with the chicken got to them before the stranger.

'Not a soul,' John Ryan said.

'Bloody clown,' Morgan said and he went to the door to see if there was a sound of a horse and cart. Hickey lifted the lid of the saucepan to show Ryan the little onions that were in it simmering. He had peeled them earlier at the outside tap and had cried buckets. It was a new saucepan that afterwards would be cleaned and put back in stock.

'How's the ladies, John?' he asked. Ryan had a great name with ladies and wasn't a bad-looking fellow. He had a long face and a longish nose and a great crop of brown, thick, curly, oily hair. His eyes were a shade of green that Hickey had never seen on any other human being, but in a shade of darning wool.

'I bet you're clicking like mad,' said Morgan coming back to the snug. He wished that he was John Ryan's age, and not a middle-aged married man with a flushed face and a scalded liver.

'I get places,' Ryan boasted, and gave a nervous laugh because he remembered his date of the night before. He had arranged to meet a girl behind the shop, on the back road which led to the creamery, the same road where Hickey had the mare and cart tethered to a gate, and where Morgan kept the logs in a stack against a wall under a tarpaulin. She'd cycled four miles to meet him because he was damned if he was going to put himself out for any girl. No sooner had she arrived than she asked him the time and said that she'd have to be thinking of getting back soon.

'Take off your scarf,' he said. She was so muffled with scarf and gloves and things that he couldn't get near her.

'I'm fine this way,' she said, standing with her bicycle between them. Half a dozen words were exchanged and she rode off again, making a date for the following Sunday night.

'So 'twas worthwhile,' Morgan said, although he had no interest in women anymore. He knew well enough that nothing much went on between men and women. His own wife nearly drove him mad, sitting in front of the kitchen fire saying she could see faces in the flames and then getting up suddenly and running upstairs to see if there was a man under her bed. He sent her to Lourdes the summer before to see if that would straighten her out but she came back worse.

'Love, it's all bull. . . .' he said. His wife had developed a craze for putting sugar and peaches into every bit of meat she cooked. Then she had a figari to buy an egg timer. She played with the egg timer at night, turning it upside down and watching the passage of the sand as it flowed down into the underneath tube. Childish she was.

'I wish he came,' Hickey said.

'Which of them?' said John Ryan.

'Long John with the chicken,' said Hickey.

'He'll be here soon, he sent word yesterday that he'd be here this morning with my Christmas box,' Morgan said.

' 'Twill be plucked and all?' John Ryan asked.

'Oh! ready for the oven,' Morgan said. 'Other years I brought it up home but I don't want it dolled up with peaches and sugar and that nonsense.'

'No man wants food ruined,' said Hickey. He pitied Morgan with the wife he had. Everyone could see she was getting more peculiar, talking to herself as she rode on her bicycle to Mass, and getting in to hide behind walls if she saw a man coming.

They heard footsteps in the shop and Ryan opened a crack in the door to see who it was.

'Is it him?'

'No, it's a young Gleeson one.'

'She can wait,' Morgan said, making no effort to get up. He was damned if he'd weigh three pennies' worth of sugar on a cold day like this. The child tapped the counter with a coin, then began to cough to let them know she was there and finally she hummed a song. In the end she had to go away unserved.

'In a month from now you'll be well away,' Hickey said.

'It's not a dead cert,' Morgan said. He had to keep some curb on his dreams because more than once he or his wife had had a promise of a legacy and were diddled out of it. Yet inwardly his spirits were soaring and made better each minute by the great draughts of whiskey which he took from the bottle. The other two men drank from mugs. In that way he was able to ration them a bit.

He had to go out to the shop for the next customer because it was the schoolteacher's maid and they gave him quite a bit of trade. She wanted particular toilet rolls for her mistress but he had none.

'Will you order them,' the maid said and Morgan made a great to-do about entering the request in the day book. Afterwards the three men had a great laugh and Morgan said it wasn't so long ago since the teacher had to use grass, but now that she was taking a correspondence course in Latin there was no stopping of her and her airs.

'And do you know,' said Hickey, although he'd probably told them before a hundred times, 'she cancels the paper if she's going away for a day, what do you think of that for meanness, a twopenny paper?'

'There he is!' said Hickey suddenly. They heard a cart being drawn up outside and a mare whinnying. Hickey knew that mare belonged to Long John Salmon because like her owner she went berserk when she got into civilised surroundings.

'Now,' said Morgan, raising his short, fat finger in warning. 'Sit tight and don't let either of you stir or he'll be in here boring us about that dead brother of his.'

Morgan went out to the shop, shook hands with Long John Salmon and wished him a Happy New Year. He was relieved to see that Long John had a rush basket under his arm, which no doubt contained the cockerel. They talked about the weather, both uttering the usual rigmarole about how bad it had been. Patches of snow still lodged in the hollows of the field across the road from the shop. The shop was situated between two villages and looked out on a big empty field with a low stone wall surrounding it. Long John said that the black frost was appalling, which was why he had to come at a snail's pace in case the mare slipped. Long John said that Christmas had been quieter than usual and Morgan agreed, though as far as he could remember, Christmas Day was always the most boring day in his married life; the pubs were closed and he was alone with his Mrs from mass-time until bed-time. This year of course she had added peaches and sugar to the turkey so there wasn't even that to enjoy.

'I had a swim Christmas Day,' Long John said. He believed in a daily swim, and flowers of sulphur on Saturdays to purify the blood.

'We had a goose but no plum pudding,' Long John added, giving Morgan the cue to hand him a small plum pudding wrapped in red glassette paper.

'Your Christmas box,' Morgan said, hoping to God Long John would hand him the chicken and get it over with. He could hear the men murmuring inside.

'Do you eat honey?' Long John asked.

'No,' said Morgan in a testy voice. He knew that Long John kept bees and had a crooked inked sign on his gate which said HONEY FOR SALE.

'No wonder you have no children,' said Long John with a grin.

Morgan was tempted to turn on him for a remark like that. He had no children not because he didn't eat honey, but because Mrs Morgan screamed the night of their honeymoon and screamed ever after when he went near her. Finally they got separate rooms.

'Well, here's a jar,' said Long John handing over a jar of honey that looked like white wax.

'That's too good altogether,' said Morgan livid with rage in case Long John was trying to do it cheap this Christmas.

'Christ Almighty,' Hickey muttered inside. 'If he doesn't hand over a chicken I'll go out in the country to his place and flog a goose.'

As if prompted, Long John then did it. He handed the chicken wrapped in newspaper, ordered some meal stuffs and said he was on his way to the forge to get the mare's shoes off.

'I'll have it all ready for you,' said Morgan almost running from the counter.

'You'd think it was a boar he was giving away,' said Hickey as Morgan came in and unwrapped the chicken.

'Don't talk to me,' said Morgan, 'get it on.'

The water had boiled away so John Ryan had to run in his patent-leather shoes to the pump, which was about a hundred yards up the road. He thought to himself that when he was a qualified doctor he'd run errands for no one, and Hickey and Morgan would be tipping their hats to him.

'It's a nice bird,' said Hickey feeling the breast, 'but you'd think he'd wrap it in butter paper.'

'Oh, a mountainy man,' said Morgan. 'What can you expect from a mountainy man.'

They put the chicken in and added lashings of salt. In twenty minutes or so it began to simmer and Morgan timed it on his pocket watch. Later Hickey put a few cubes of Oxo in the water to flavour the soup. Morgan was demented from explaining to customers that all he was cooking was a sheep's head for a dog. Hickey and John Ryan sat tight in the snug and smoked ten cigarettes apiece. Hickey got it out of John Ryan that the girl of the night before was a waste of time. He liked knowing these things because although he did not have many dates with girls, he liked to be sure that a girl was amenable.

'I didn't get within a mile of her,' John Ryan said and regretted telling it two seconds later. He had his name to keep up and most of the local men thought that because of being a medical student he did extraordinary things with girls and took terrible risks.

'I didn't fancy her anyhow,' John Ryan said, 'I've had too many women lately, women have no shame in them nowadays.'

'Ah, stop,' said Hickey, hoping that John Ryan would tell him some juicy incidents about orgies in Dublin and street walkers who wore nothing under their dresses. At that moment Morgan came in from the shop and said they ought to have a drop of the soup. He was getting irritable because he had been so busy at the counter and the whiskey was going to his head and fuddling him.

'If I could begin my life again I'd be in the demolition business,' Morgan said for no reason. He imagined that there must be great satisfaction in destroying houses, and breaking

up ornamental mantelshelfs and smashing windows. He sometimes had a dream in which Mrs Morgan lay under a load of
mortar and white rubble, with her clothes well above her knees.
Hickey got three new cups from the shop and lifted out the soup
with one of them. By now the stove was so hot that dribbles of
spilt soup sizzled on the black iron top. It was the finest soup
any of them had ever tasted.

'Whoever comes in now can wait, 'cos I'm not budging,'
Morgan said, as he sat on the principal chair and drank the soup
noisily. It was at that very moment Hickey said 'Wisht', and a
car was heard to pull up. The three of them were at the door
instantly, and saw the rather battered V8 come to a halt close to
the wall. The driver was a small butty fellow with red hair and
red beard.

'Oh Red Hugh of the North,' said Hickey casting
aspersions on the car and the rust on the radiator.

'I don't like his attire,' said John Ryan.

The man wore no jacket but a greyish jersey that looked
like a dishcloth, as it was full of holes.

'Shag his attire,' said Morgan and went forward to greet
the stranger, and apologise for the state of the weather. It had
begun to rain or rather to hail and the snow in the field was being
turned to slime. The stranger winked at the three of them and
gave a little toss of the head to denote how sporting he was. He
was by far the smallest of them. He spoke in the clipped accent
of the North and they could see at once that he was briary. He
seemed to be looking at them severely as if he was mentally
assessing their characters.

'Matt O'Meara's the name,' he said shaking hands with
Morgan, but merely nodding to the others. In the snug he was
handed a large whiskey without being asked whether he was
teetotal or not. He made them uneasy with his silence and his
staring blue eyes.

'Knock that back,' Morgan said, 'and then we'll talk
turkey.'

He winked at John Ryan. Ryan was briefed to open the
proceedings by telling the fellow how rain played havoc with

every damned thing, even gates, and how one didn't know whether it was the oxygen or the hydrogen or some trace minerals that did such damage.

'You'd ask yourself what they add to the rain,' Ryan said and secretly congratulated himself for his erudition.

'Like what the Priest said about the French cheese,' said Hickey, but Morgan did not want Hickey to elaborate on that bloody story before they got things sorted out. It would have been better if Hickey had been given porter because he had no head for spirits.

'Well, we have the hay-sheds,' Morgan said and the man smiled coldly as if that was a foregone conclusion.

'How many have you contracted?' the man asked. He showed no courtesy but Morgan thought business is business and tolerated it.

'If we get the gentlemen farmers, the others will follow suit,' Morgan said.

'How many gentlemen farmers are there?' the fellow asked and by doing a quick count and with much interruption and counter-interruption from Ryan and Hickey it was concluded that there were at least twenty gentlemen farmers. The man did his sums on the back of his hand with the stub of a pencil and said that that would yield a thousand pounds and stared icily at his future partners. Five hundred each. Morgan could not repress a smile and already in his mind he had reserved the hackney car for Friday and Saturday evenings. He asked if by any chance the man had brought a sample and was told no. There were dozens of hay-sheds in the North where it had been used and if Morgan wanted to go up there and vet them he was quite welcome. This man had a very abrasive manner.

'If you want, I can go elsewhere,' he said.

Hickey saw that the fellow could become obstreperous and, sensing a rift, he said that if they were going to be partners they must all shake on it, and they did.

'Comrades,' said the fellow much to their astonishment. They abhorred that word. Stalin used that word and a woman in

South America called Eva Peron. It was the moment for Morgan to remind Hickey to produce the eats as their visitor must be starving. Hickey sharpened the knife, drew up his sleeves and began to carve like an expert. He resolved to give Ryan and the visitor a leg each and keep the breast for himself and Morgan. Up at Brady's where he worked for seventeen years he had never tasted a bit of the breast. She always gave it to her husband even though he drank acres of arable land away, threatened to kill her more than once and indeed might have, only that he, Hickey had intervened and swiped the revolver or pitchfork or whatever weapon Brady had to hand. The stranger, deferring food, began to ask a few practical questions such as where they would get lodging, whose hay-shed they ought to do first, and where he could store the ladders and various equipment if they came on the Sunday. The plan was that himself and his two men would arrive at the weekend and start on the Monday. Morgan said he would get them fixed up in digs, and it was agreed that pest though she was, Mrs Gleeson wasn't such a bad landlady, being liberal with tea and cake at any hour. The stranger then enquired about the fishing and set Hickey off on a rigmarole about eels.

'We'll take you on the lake when the May fly is up,' Morgan said and boasted about his boat that was moored down at the pier.

'There is one thing,' said the stranger. 'It's the deposit.' He smiled as he said this and pursed his lips.

Morgan, who was extremely cordial up to then looked sour and stared at the newcomer with disbelief. 'Do you think I came up the river on a bicycle.'

'I don't,' said the stranger, 'but do *you* think I came up the river on a bicycle', and then very matter of factly he explained that three men, the lorry, the gallons of the expensive stuff and equipment had to be carted from the North. He then reminded them that farmers all over Ireland were crying out for his services. A brazen fellow he was. 'I want a hundred pounds,' he said.

'That's a fortune,' said Hickey.

'I'll give you fifty,' said Morgan flatly, only to be told that it wasn't worth a tinker's curse, that if Morgan & Co. preferred he would gladly take his business elsewhere. Morgan saw that he had no alternative, so he slowly moved to the safe and undid the creaky brass catch.

'That needs oiling,' said Hickey, pointlessly. The place seethed with tension and bad feeling.

The money was in small brown envelopes and the notes were kept together with rubber bands, some of them shredding. Morgan did not go to the bank often as it only gave people the wrong idea. He did not even like this villain watching him as he parted them and counted.

The man did not seem either embarrassed or exhilarated at receiving the money, he simply made a poor joke about its being dirty. He confirmed the arrangements and said to make only two appointments for the first week in case the weather was bad or there was any other hitch. He put the money into an old mottled wallet and said he'd be off. Despite the fact that Morgan had provided eats he did not press the fellow to stay. He did not like him. They'd have a better time of it themselves so he was quite pleased to mouth formalities and shake hands coldly with the blackguard.

Once he had gone they fled to the snug to devour their dinner and discuss him. John Ryan took an optimistic view, pointing out that he did not want to slinge and was therefore a solid worker. Hickey said that for a small butty he wasn't afraid to stand up to people, but that wasn't it significant that he hadn't cracked a joke. Hickey could see that Morgan was a bit on edge so he thought to bolster him.

'Anyhow he'll bring in the spondoolicks,' and he reminded Morgan to make a note of the fact that he had paid him a hundred pounds as if Morgan could forget. Morgan dipped the plain pen in the bottle of ink and asked aloud what date it was, though he knew it already.

No sooner had they sat down to eat than John Ryan started sniffing. Every forkful was put to his nose before being consigned to his mouth. Hickey commented on this and on the fact that John Ryan wouldn't eat a shop egg if you paid him.

'It doesn't smell right,' John Ryan said.

'God's sake it's the tastiest chicken I ever ate,' Hickey said.

'First class, first class,' Morgan said though he didn't fancy it that much. That blackguard had depressed him and hadn't given him any sense of comradeship but hooked it soon as he got the hundred pounds. Had the others not been there Morgan would have haggled and he resolved in future to do business alone.

'Are you in, Morgan?' They heard Long John Salmon call from the shop and sullenly Morgan got up and put his plate of dinner on top of the stove.

'Coming,' he said as he wiped his mouth.

Out in the shop he asked Long John if he had any other calls to do, because business had been so brisk he hadn't got around to weighing the meal stuff.

'Nicest chicken I ever had,' he then said humouring Long John.

'They're a good table fowl, the Rhode Islands,' said Long John.

'They are,' said Morgan, 'they're the best.'

'If I'd known you were eating it so soon I'd have got it all ready for you,' said Long John.

'It *was* ready, hadn't a thing to do only put it in the pot with some onions and salt and Bob's your uncle.'

''Twasn't cleaned,' said Long John Salmon.

'What?' said Morgan, not fully understanding.

'Christ, that's what it is,' said John Ryan, dropping his plate and making one leap out of the snug and through the shop, around to the back where he could be sick.

'He's in a hurry,' said Long John as he saw Ryan go out with his hand clapped across his mouth.

'You mean it wasn't drawn,' said Morgan and he felt queasy. Then he remembered being in Long John's farmyard

and he writhed as he contemplated the muck of the place.
Sorrows never come in single file. At that moment Guard Tighe
came into the shop in uniform, looking agitated.

'Was there a bloke here about spraying hay-sheds?' he
asked.

'What business is it of yours,' Morgan said.

Morgan was thinking that Tighe was nosey and probably
wanted the franchise for his wife's people who had a hardware
shop up the street.

'Was he or wasn't he?'

'He was here,' said Morgan and he was on the point of
boasting of his new enterprise when the Guard forestalled him.

'He's a bounder,' he said. 'He's going all over the country
bamboozling people.'

'How do you know that?' Morgan said.

Hickey had come from inside the snug, wild with
curiosity.

'I know it because the man who invented the damn stuff
got in touch with us, warning us about this bounder, this
pretender.'

'Jaysus,' said Morgan. 'Why didn't you tell me sooner.'

'We're a guard short,' said Tighe, and at that instant
Morgan hit the counter with his fist and kept hitting it so that
billheads and paper bags flew about.

'You're supposed to protect citizens,' he said.

'You didn't give him any money?' said the Guard.

'Only *one hundred pounds*,' said Morgan with vehemence,
as if the Guard was the cause of it all, instead of his own
importunity. The Guard then asked particulars of the car, the
licence plate, the man's appearance, dismissing the man's name
as fictitious. When the Guard asked if the man's beard looked to
be dyed, Morgan lost his temper completely and called upon his
Maker to wreak vengeance on embezzlers, chancers, bounders,
thieves, layabouts, liars and the Garda Siotchana.

'Christ I didn't even give myself a Christmas box,' Morgan
said, and Hickey sensing that worse was to follow picked up his
cap and said it was heinous, heinous altogether. Outside he

found Ryan, white as a sheet, over near the wall where the mare and cart were tethered.

'Red Hugh of the North was a bounder,' he said.

'I don't care what he was,' said Ryan predicting his own demise.

'You're very chicken,' said Hickey thrilled at making such an apt joke.

'If you had stayed inside I was all right,' said Ryan as he commenced to retch again. Hickey looked up and saw that Mrs Gleeson was crouched behind the other side of the wall observing. In her black garb she looked like a witch. She'd tell the whole country.

'She'll tell my mother,' said Ryan and drew his coat collar up around him to try and disguise his appearance.

'Good, good Bess,' Hickey said to the mare as he unknotted the reins. Morgan had come out and like a lunatic was waving his arms in all directions and calling for action. Hickey was damned if he was going to stay for any post mortem. It was obvious that the whole thing was a swindle and the fellow was now in some smart hotel eating his fill or more likely heading for the boat to Holyhead. Exit the gangsters.

'Get rid of this bloody chicken,' Morgan called.

'Add peaches to it,' said Hickey.

'Come back,' said Morgan. 'Come back you hooligan.'

But Hickey had already set out and the mare was trotting at a merry pace having been unaccountably idle for a couple of hours.

The Doll

Every Christmas there came a present of a doll from a lady I scarcely knew. She was a friend of my mother's and though they only met rarely, or accidentally at a funeral, she kept up the miraculous habit of sending to me a doll. It would come on the evening bus shortly before Christmas and it added to the hectic glow of those days when everything was charged with bustle and excitement. We made potato stuffing, we made mince pies, we made bowls of trifle, we decorated the window sills with holly and with tinsel, and it was as if untoward happiness was about to befall us.

Each year's doll seemed to be more beautiful, more bewitching and more sumptuously clad than the previous year's. They were of both sexes. There was a jockey in bright red and saffron, there was a Dutch drummer boy in maroon velvet, there was a sleeping doll in a crinoline, a creature of such fragile beauty that I used to fear for her when my sisters picked her up clumsily or tried to make her flutter her eyelashes. Her eyes were suggestive of china and small blue flowers, having the haunting colour of one and the smooth glaze of the other. She was named Rosalind.

My sisters, of course, were jealous and riled against the unfairness of my getting a doll whereas they only got the usual dull flannel sock with tiny things in it, necessary things such as pencils, copybooks, plus some toffees and a liquorice pipe. Each of my dolls was given a name, and a place of rest, in a corner or on a whatnot, or in an empty biscuit tin, and each had special conversations allotted to them, special endearments, and if necessary special chastisements. They had special times for fresh air — a doll would be brought out and splayed on a window sill, or sunk down in the high grass and apparently abandoned. I had no favourites until the seventh doll came and she was to me the living representation of a princess. She too was a sleeping doll but a sizeable one and she was dressed in a pale-blue dress, with a gauze overdress, a pale-blue bonnet and white kid button shoes. My sisters – who were older – were as smitten with her as I. She was uncanny. We all agreed that she was almost lifelike and that with coaxing she might speak. Her flaxen hair was like a feather to finger, her little wrists moved on a swivel, her eyelashes were black and sleek and the gaze in her eyes so fetching that we often thought she was not an inanimate creature, that she had a soul, and a sense of us. Conversations with her were the most intense and the most incriminating of all.

It so happened that the teacher at school harboured a dislike for me and this for unfathomable reasons. I loved lessons, was first with my homework, always early for class, then always lit the school fire, raked the ashes, and had a basket full of turf and wood when she arrived. In fact my very diligence was what annoyed her and she would taunt me about it and proclaim what a 'goody-goody' I was. She made jokes about my cardigan or my shoe laces or the slide in my hair and to make the other girls laugh she referred to me as 'It'. She would say 'It has a hole in its sock', or 'It hasn't got a proper blazer', or 'It has a daub on its copybook.' I believe she hated me. If in an examination I came first – and I usually did – she would read out everyone's marks, leave mine until last and say, 'We know who swotted the most', as if I were in disgrace. If at cookery classes I made pancakes and offered her one she would make a face as if I had offered her tripe or strychnine. She once got a big girl to give me fruit laxatives pretending that they were sweets and made great fun when I had to go in and out to the closets all day. It was a cruel cross to bear. When the Inspector came and praised me she said that I was brainy but that I lacked versatility. In direct contrast she was lovely to my sisters and would ask them occasionally how was my mother, and when was she going to send over a nice pot of homemade jam or a slab cake. I used to pray and make novenas that one day she would examine her conscience and think on how she wronged me and repent.

One day my prayers seemed on the point of being answered. It was November and already the girls were saving up for Christmas and we knew that soon there would be the turkey market and soon after hams and little seedless oranges in the grocery shop window. She said that since we'd all done so well in the Catechism exam she was going to get the infants to act in the school play and that we would build a crib and stack it with fresh hay and statues. Somebody said that my doll would make a most beautiful Virgin. Several girls had come home with me to see the doll and had been allowed to peep in at her in her box that was lined with silver chaff. I brought her next day and every head in the classroom craned as the teacher lifted the lid of the black lacquered box and looked in.

'She's passable,' she said, and told one of the girls to put the doll in the cookery press until such time as she was needed. I grieved at being parted from her but I was proud of the fact that she would be in the school play and be the cynosure of all. I had made her a cloak, a flowing blue cloak with a sheath of net over it and a little diamante clasp. She was like a creature of moonlight, shimmering, even on dark wet days. The cookery press was not a fit abode for her but what could I do?

The play did not pass off without incident. The teacher's cousin, Milo, was drunk, belligerent and offensive. He called girls up to the fire to pretend to talk to them and then touched the calves of their legs and tickled the backs of their knees. He called me up and asked would I click. He was an auctioneer from the city and unmarried. The teacher's two sons also came to look at the performance but one of them left in the middle. He was strange and would laugh for no reason and although over twenty he called the teacher 'Mammy'. He had very bright red hair and a peculiar stare in his eyes. For the most part the infants forgot their lines, lost their heads and the prompter was always late so that the wrong girls picked up her cues. She was behind a curtain but could be heard out on the street. The whole thing was a fiasco. My doll was the star of the occasion and everyone raved about her.

Afterwards there was tea and scones and the teacher talked to those few mothers who had come. My mother had not come because at that time she was unable to confront crowds and even dreaded going to Mass on Sundays, but believed that God would preserve her from the dizziness and suffocations that she was suffering from. After they had all left and a few of us had done the washing up, I went to the teacher and to my delight she gave me a wide genial smile. She thanked me for the doll, said that there was no denying but that the doll saved the play and then as I reached out she staved my hand with a ruler and laughed heartily.

'You don't think I'm going to let you have her now, I've got quite fond of her . . . the little mite,' she said and gave the china cheek a tap. At home I was berserk. My mother said the teacher was probably teasing and that she would return the doll in a day or two. My father said that if she didn't she would have to answer to him, or else get a hammering. The days passed and the holidays came and not only did she not give me my doll but she took it to her own home and put it in the china cabinet along with cups and ornaments. Passing by their window I would look in. I could not see her because the china cabinet was in a corner, but I knew where she was as the maid Lizzie told me. I would press my forehead to the window and call to the doll and say that I was thinking of her, and that rescue was being hatched.

Everyone agreed that it was monstrous but no one talked to the teacher, no one tackled her. The truth is they were afraid of her. She had a bitter tongue and also, being superstitious, they felt that she could give us children brains or take them away as a witch might. It was as if she could lift the brains out of us with a forceps and pickle them in brine. No one did anything and in time I became reconciled to it. I asked once in a fit of bravura and the teacher said wasn't I becoming impudent. No longer did I halt to look in the window of her house but rather crossed the road and I did not talk to Lizzie in case she should tell me something upsetting.

Once I was sent to the teacher's house with a loin of pork and found her by the fire with her queer son, both of them with their stockings down, warming themselves. There were zigzags of heat on their shins. She asked if I wanted to go in and see the doll, but I declined. By then I was preparing to go away to boarding school and I knew that I would be free of her for ever, that I would forget her, that I would forget the doll, forget most of what happened, or at least remember it without a quiver.

The years go by and everything and everyone gets replaced. Those we knew, though absent, are yet merged inextricably into new folk so that each person is to us a sum of many others and the effect is of opening box after box in which the original is forever hidden.

The teacher dies a slow death, wastes to a thread through cancer, yet strives against it and says she is not ready. I hear the amount of money she left and her pitiable last words but I feel nothing. I feel none of the rage and none of the despair. She does not matter to me any more. I am on the run from them. I have fled. I live in a city. I am cosmopolitan. People come to my house, all sorts of people, and they do feats like dancing, or jesting, or singing, inventing a sort of private theatre where we all play a part. I too play a part. My part is to receive them and disarm them, ply them with food and drink and secretly be wary of them, be distanced from them. Like them I smile, and drift, like them I smoke or drink to induce a feverishness or a pleasant wandering hallucination. It is not something I cultivated. It developed of its own accord, like a spore that breathes in the darkness. So I am far from those I am with, and far from those I have left. At night I enjoy the farness. In the morning I touch a table or a teacup to make sure that it is a table or a teacup and I talk to it, and I water the flowers and I talk to them, and I think how tender flowers are, and woods and woodsmoke and possibly how tender are my new friends but that like me they are intent on concealment. None of us ever says where we come from or what haunts us. Perhaps we are bewildered or ashamed.

I go back. Duty hauls me back to see the remaining relatives and I play the expected part. I had to call on the teacher's son. He was the undertaker and was in charge of my aunt's burial. I went to pay him, to 'fix up' as it is called, and his wife whom I knew to be a bit scattered admitted me amidst peals of laughter. She said she always thought I had jet-black hair, as she ran down the hall calling his name. His name is Denis. He shakes hands with me very formally, asks what kind of wreath I want and if it should be heart-shaped, circular, or in the form of a cross. I leave it all to him. There in the over-stuffed china cabinet is my confiscated doll and if dolls can age, it certainly had done. Grey and mouldy, the dress and cloak are as a shroud and I thought if I were to pick her up she would disintegrate.

'God, my mother was fond of her,' he said, as if he were trying to tell me that she had been fond of me too. Had he said so I might have hissed. I was older now and it was clear to me that she had kept the doll out of perversity, out of pique and jealousy. In some way she had divined that I would have a life far away from them and adventures such as she herself would never taste. Sensing my chill, he boasted that he had not let his own children play with the doll, thereby implying that she was a sacred object, a treasured souvenir. He hauled out a brandy bottle and winked expecting me to say yes. I declined.

A sickness had come over me, a sort of nausea for having cared so much about the doll, for having let them maltreat me and now for no longer caring at all. My abrupt departure puzzled him. He did something untoward. He tried to kiss me. He thought perhaps that in my world it was the expected thing. Except that the kiss was proffered as a sympathy kiss, a kiss of condolence over my aunt's death. His face had the sour smell of a towel that he must have dried himself on, just before he came to welcome me. The kiss was clumsiness personified. I pitied him but I could not stay, and I could not reminisce, and I could not pretend to be the fast kiss-easy woman he imagined me to be.

Walking down the street, where I walk in memory, morning noon and night, I could not tell what it was, precisely, that reduced me to such wretchedness. Indeed it was not death but rather the gnawing conviction of not having yet lived. All I could tell was that the stars were as singular and as wondrous as I remembered them and that they still seemed like a link, an enticement to the great heavens, and that one day I would reach them and be absorbed into their glory, and pass from a world that, at that moment, I found to be rife with cruelty and stupidity, a world that had forgotten how to give.

'Tomorrow . . .' I thought. 'Tomorrow I shall be gone', and realised that I had not lost the desire to escape or the strenuous habit of hoping.

The Bachelor

In the distance he was often mistaken for a priest so solemn did he seem in his great long black overcoat and his black squashed hat. His face was grave too and very often he had a drip at the end of his pointed nose. It was unusual to see a grown man with tears in his eyes and this even when he told something light-hearted. The tears would start up in his eyes almost as soon as he began to talk, giving him a morose funereal look. He wore striped flannelette shirts and a tattered homespun jacket that he had once shared with his dead brother. When his brother was alive they had to attend Mass separately as each wanted to be the proud wearer of the oatmeal jacket.

I used to catch fleas for him and keep them in a match box and my reward was a penny and a glass of raspberry wine. Nothing can, or could, ever quell the thrill of seeing the thick red cordial in the bottom of a tumbler, and then the flurry as he shot out to the yard where the tap was, and then the leisurely joy of watching him dilute it, of watching its redness gradually pale and pale until it was a beautiful light aerated pink, and oh, for its taste, so sweet and so synthetic, that it even surpassed the joyous taste of warm, melting jelly. I don't know what he did with the fleas but I know that my mother was incensed when she heard of it and forbade me to catch any more, deeming it a disgrace.

Jack owned a wine shop which he called a 'Taverna'. It was dark and huge like a barracks, and even in the daytime, when devoid of customers, the air reeked with the smell of stale flat porter, just as the high oak counter had the circular marks of thousands of porter glasses, laid down in different humours, in rage, in mirth, and quite often in insupportable melancholia.

Jack did not do brisk business but certain men went there when they wanted to drink quietly and purposefully, and at night a particular crowd went, preferring it to the neighbouring bars because there was no woman to harangue them, or gossip, or tell the whole country how much they drank, or what they owed. Jack's sister Maggie was an invalid, and lived her days hunched over the kitchen fire, occasionally letting out a moan that sounded like a prayer and alerting him to the fact if a sod fell onto the floor or if she was in need of tea. My mother sometimes took pity on them and sent a gift of a cake, or black puddings, or a pot of marmalade in the spring when the oranges came from Seville and the women vied with each other as to whose marmalade was the most tempting. Jack would hasten to our house, and thank her with extravagant phrases, but suddenly unable to conquer his awkwardness, he would just lift his hat and run away. He loved my mother and used to stroll in our fields to catch sight of her. In the summer mornings on my way to school I would find him, as he said, penning a little ode. One morning when the horse chestnut tree was in flower and the beautiful cream blooms hung like candles, merely waiting to be lit, I came on him reciting excitedly. The brightness and the freshness of the morning, the rustle of the trees, birds scurrying about and all of nature hell bent on its bacchanalia must have fired him as greatly as did his secret passion, and all this despite the fact that he was a grown man who had never probably known a hand clasp or certainly a kiss.

'Just penning a little poem,' he said.

'What sort of poem?' I asked.

'Ah, you're too young to know,' he said and then enquired if my mother ever came down this far.

'Only to follow turkeys,' I said, and he moved off muttering to himself and smiling in a bemused way. I guessed that the poem was composed in Latin which no one would be likely to read, or translate, not even a clerical student, because Jack's Latin was a botch, gleaned partly from his missal and richly embellished. I could have told him that the written word did not move my mother, that she never read anything, only the price of eggs in the daily paper and the big, stained Mrs Beeton cookery book. Moreover she believed that books were sinful, that poetry was rubbish and that such things helped to turn people's minds and deflect them from their true work. I did not tell him, though I do not know why, since it was my habit to blurt.

The following Sunday when I was going into Mass, Jack grabbed my coat sleeve and whispered that he would call on us that night as he had a surprise for me. My mother used always Sunday evenings to soak her feet in hot water and washing soda and then to pare her corns with my father's razor blade. It was a formidable and frightening sight. My father usually went to play cards though it was something we could not afford, being heavily in debt. But after she had done her feet she smiled a little and said, 'To hell with it', but that she felt like dolling up. So seldom did she ever dress up that it was almost akin to a ceremony to follow her upstairs, go into the Blue Room, see her open the wardrobe and touch the few long dresses that despite their age and their musty smell still conjured up pictures of all-night dances, buffet suppers, music and merriment. She put on her white georgette blouse which had patches of vivid red flowers embroidered on the bodice, and a drawstring which could either be tied tightly or allowed to go slack. She did not tie the string very tightly and the effect was perfect, her pale neck, the white gauzy material, and the magic of the flowers such that it seemed they might stir like flowers in a garden. Downstairs, in the kitchen we lit the lamp and her hair which was red-brown glinted as she proceeded to make sandwiches from the bacon left over from lunch. I thought then that when I grew up if I could be as fetching as my mother I would be certain to find happiness. For some reason I believed that the troubles of her life were an anomaly and never did it occur to me that some of her fatality had already grafted itself onto me and determined my disposition.

'Is there company coming?' I asked.

'Hardly,' she said, 'I expect Jack was only raving.'

Yet she showed no surprise when the familiar knock came on the back door and she jumped to answer it. Jack came in, looked about but would not take off his hat, he merely lifted it slightly to salute us. We felt sorry for him because he was ashamed of his bald scalp and people said that not one hair grew on it and that it was the colour of putty. He took a tin from his pocket and handed it to me with a flourish. It had a picture of a couple on a jaunting car and inside there were boiled sweets that had adhered together with dirt and the dried sugar. Once one sucked them they tasted of cloves, as they should. He sat down and gradually started to draw his chair nearer to my mother as he began to expound.

'Strange to say, Mrs O, I was looking forward to my little expedition here, and unfortunately I was detained, a very irksome thing when one prides oneself on one's punctuality.'

'It's early, Jack,' my mother said flatly.

'The maternity nurse, Mrs O . . .'

On hearing this my mother made a face that conveyed her disgust. She had an idea that all nurses were crude, but the maternity nurse was the limit altogether as she insisted on describing women's labours and the different ways their water broke.

'Trying to get yours truly into her clutches, Mrs O,' he said, drawing his chair dangerously near. Their bodies were at an angle to each other and I thought that if he moved nearer they would have to touch.

'Makes no secret of her intentions,' he said and then he whispered something which must have been wanton, because my mother writhed and put on her injured face.

'I like a woman to be a lady,' he said and he smiled at her in the most bashful but apparent way and at that instant she jumped up and said she was dying for an apple. The tiled floor of the vestibule was covered with small wrinkled wine-coloured apples and these gave a delicious smell to the whole house and even the rotting ones made one long for stewed apple or a pie. She returned with a dishful of apples and taking a small knife from the kitchen drawer she peeled one and gave it to Jack, then she peeled another, and then she sat on the far side of the fire, a distance away from him.

'By the way, Mrs O,' he paused as he munched, 'there's a little gift awaiting you in my Taverna. Drop in at your convenience.'

'Oh Jack, you're too good!' she said and she beamed at him and I was sure that now she was sorry for having rebuffed him earlier. As she stood up to make the tea Jack got up too, dropped three apple pips down inside her low-cut blouse and fled from the kitchen muttering something about his sister's swooning fits.

'Can't you stay, Jack, and have a cup,' she said, but he had already lifted the heavy latch and was gone. She sent me after him with the flashlamp. I saw his figure going down the field but I didn't call after him because I hated him using our cups and being so personal with my mother. It was dark and hushed outside and I could hear the cows and the horses cropping the grass and from the village came the strains of a piano accordion playing 'Danny Boy'. I was unsettled for some reason and came inside followed by the three sheepdogs who whined for bread and who would not leave the kitchen until they received a crust each.

'He's gone,' I said.

'Creature,' she said, 'gone home to nothing only tea and loaf bread and poor Maggie rambling.'

'I wonder what's the present,' I said.

'That's what I was wondering,' she said and I could see that she was intrigued.

'Would you prefer him to Dada?' I asked and at that very moment my father came in. To my surprise Mama told him that he shouldn't have been so long and that she was bored to tears with Jack who insisted on telling her smutty stories.

'Bloody clown, who asked him here anyhow,' my father said, then shouted and stamped the floor with his boot, a thing he always did to give impetus to his bad temper. He was jealous. I saw it in his wild unsatiated protruding eyes, but I did not know what to call it then.

'I'll have that cold meat, I'm hungry,' he said peremptorily.

'I made sandwiches,' she said, placatingly.

'Damn your sandwiches, a man gets no satisfaction in this house,' and suddenly he banged the table with his fist and sent the dish of apples flying.

'Get me my light shoes,' he said to me and I fetched them from the shoe closet and threw them on the ground near where he stood. I thought I smelt whiskey and then put the thought aside as being just fear, imaginary fear, but Mama thought it too, and that night in bed we both prayed and cried hoping that he would not go on a batter.

The next evening when I got home from school there was a note propped against the tea caddy to say that I was to keep a kettle boiling as she had gone down to Jack's to collect her gift. I sat by the window and watched for her and when I saw the gleam of her bicycle coming in at the gate I ran down the fields eager to know what she had been given, envisaging a georgette scarf or a beaded bag.

'You'll catch cold without a coat,' she shouted from halfway up the field.

'What did you get?' I called.

When she was close to me I saw the disappointment. It was a packet of coffee beans and utterly useless as we never drank coffee and moreover we had nothing to grind the beans with.

'You were ages,' I said.

'I was looking at jewellery, gorgeous brooches belonging to Maggie, upstairs in a box.'

'Were you upstairs?' I said. There was something untoward about that.

'Yes, and you should see the bedroom.' She raised her eyes pitifully, towards the sky, to emphasise the squalor.

'Bare boards and not a thing in his room only an iron bed with his rosary beads hanging at the head of it and his good suit on a chair.'

She seemed to be very disgruntled and when we went in

she threw the coffee beans into a holdall where we kept useless things, bottle tops, bits of used string, and a rusted tin opener.

Two days later when I came home from school there was a car outside our front door and I quickened thinking it was visitors. But as I approached the house I heard shouting and knew once again that we were in trouble.

'You poor child you,' my mother said, hugging me and then she told me that the Bailiff was inside with my father and that unless we could find money we could be out on the roadside with the tinkers. At that moment the Bailiff came into the kitchen and said he wanted a drink of water. He had a bad stomach and was obliged to take tablets every few hours. She offered him tea which he declined and he just stood there, frowning as if he could not comprehend why people like us with a nice house and furniture had come to such desperately unhappy straits. She offered tea a second time and I think he was annoyed that she should mix up hospitality with the odious business on hand. It was then he realised that I was there and perhaps feeling sorry for me he asked suddenly, 'Who's the best at school?'

'I am,' I said not knowing that I was boasting.

Then the Sergeant arrived and my mother begged him to go in and get the revolver from my father. All three of them went in. I looked through the jamb of the door and saw my father standing near the mantelpiece, the revolver in his hand, his hat thrown back on his head and his mouth frothing. It was like a man in a picture, depicting danger. They were trying to reason with him and the more they tried, the more he foamed. Suddenly my mother left the room and said she would be back in a matter of minutes. She cycled down the drive with a wizard speed and presently she was back accompanied by Jack. She handed the Bailiff a brown envelope containing a wad of money. Then the Sergeant linked my father and helped him upstairs and though my father fell a few times he never lost grip of the bottle of whiskey that had a label with two shades of gold on it. After the Sergeant left, Jack stayed with us and spoke about the vale of tears and life's tribulations. Then when my father was asleep Jack took off his boots and stole upstairs to get the revolver from under the pillow. Also he emptied most of the whiskey into a jug and filled the whiskey bottle with water. Mama put the retrieved whiskey into a lemonade bottle saying she would keep it for the Christmas cake. The kitchen was foul with the smell.

'Well Mrs O, you know who your friends are, you can rely on Jack,' and then he tied his boots and took his leave. Mama stood on the step with him and he said something to which her reply baffled me.

'How could I, Jack,' she said pityingly and then she came back into the kitchen and asked God Almighty what would become of us. She talked of my sisters and brother who were at boarding school and said with no money for fees they would no doubt be expelled, and have to come home to rough it. I said that when I grew up I would be rich and that I would install us all in a big house where there would be no wrangling and no debt.

'You'll be lucky if you have any education,' she said dolefully and then conjectured about the impossibility of refunding Jack.

'He won't mind,' I said but she was not so sure about that. She said paupers were paupers and people soon wearied of them. The word pauper sounded so beautiful like some kind of Indian flower or fruit. Later when we heard my father shout we ran out of the house and hid in a hollow behind some trees until he had gone. We well knew the pattern, which was that he would be missing for days and eventually he would be taken to hospital and then he would come home and apologise for everything.

He came home about two weeks later and asked me to come and count his horses with him. I hated going. It had rained a lot and the fields had pools of water in which the clouds were reflected and kept appearing and disappearing. There were three horses and a young foal. I feared them as much as I feared him because they too stood for unpredictability and massive jerky strength. As we went to the field they came towards us whinnying, and I kept lurking behind for shelter.

'They won't touch you, they won't touch you,' he said as the horse kicked the ground with her hoof as if in a temper. First they galloped wildly but after a bit they quietened down, and nuzzled to see if he had brought any oats.

'I'm a good father, good to you and your mother.'

'You're not,' I thought but did not speak.

'Answer me,' he said.

'Yes,' I said grudgingly, and he went on to say that the reason for his recent little mishap was that he did not like the way Jack Holland was making free with my mother. He said it was a disgrace and that it would have to end. I said nothing. By now the horses on a whim had all decided to lie down in the pools of water and roll around so that they became covered in mud, their haunches smeared. They hadn't seen a soul for two weeks and were probably complaining about this, by resorting to antics. Next day Mama wrote Jack a letter and marked it personal. She put SAG (St Anthony Guide) on the back of the envelope and dispatched me with it. It was my first time in Jack's kitchen. It was a large kitchen with a stone floor and a great hearth fire. There was a smell of fried onions, wet turf and old ashes. Maggie was dozing in a rocking chair by the fire and Jack was having a mug of tea at the kitchen table.

'Have a little repast,' he said as I went in. To read the letter he had to borrow his sister's glasses, so he pulled them off her face and put them on his own. They were rimless glasses and made him look penurious. A few hens had come in from the yard and were picking at a colander in which there had been cold cabbage but was now almost picked clean. They were very intent on this. A sprig of faded palm was stuck beside the globe of the Sacred Heart lamp and I reckoned that it had been there since Easter. The willow-patterned plates that were wedged into the dresser badly needed a wash. I tried to find a disappointed look on his face as he read the letter but there was none.

'Tell your Mam that Jack understands all, and that Jack

will wait for time's eventualities,' and I said I would, and ran out of the kitchen because I had some idea that he was going to kiss me. After that he visited us rarely, and when he did he talked mostly to Dada. But often on the way from school he called me by rapping the windows with his knuckles.

'How's your Mam?'

'She's well.'

Even when she wasn't, I said it out of deference. Then he'd put two bars of chocolate in an envelope and send them to her.

I was twelve when Maggie died, and we all sat in the parlour, and the ladies drank port wine and nibbled marietta biscuits. Jack looked sad, a drip on his nose and a black diamond of cloth on the sleeve of his brown jacket. The maternity nurse sewed it on for him.

'Creature.'

'How many years is it at all since she got crippled?'

'She was lucky to have Jack.'

'She's gone straight to Heaven.'

They all said the same things, agreed with each other about Maggie's sainthood and probably dimly thought of their own deaths. My mother said that she would make tea and no doubt she was impelled to do it, so as to keep my father from anything alcoholic. In the parlour where she and I went to get the cups we found dog daisies in a jug on the sideboard with the water putrid and the daisies themselves shrivelled up. She said what was a house without a woman, and as she carried the jug out, the women had to put their handkerchiefs or their gloved hands to their noses. As we walked home she told my father this and said it was a pity that Jack had never married and that perhaps he would now.

'Whoever marries Jack will have Maggie's brooches,' I said.

'Maybe he'll wait for you,' she said jokingly.

'She'll marry a doctor,' said my father proudly, as he hoped that I would better their situation.

'She'll marry Jack,' my mother said and the thought was offensive. It happened to be a time when my girl friends and I secretly talked of nothing but marriage. We skipped to a rhyme that went:

Raspberry strawberry blackberry jam
tell me the name of my young man.

and we mused on the film stars who were our idols. So many girls plumped for Clark Gable that several were insanely jealous of each other and if one said 'Clark', another would say 'Excuse me, are you talking of my friend Clark Gable', and enmity ensued. Daisies were plucked, novenas were said and spells resorted to. There was one spell that surpassed all others for novelty. In the post came that particular little white box lined with silver paper that contained dark rich wedding cake, so dense with different fruits that it was as if it had no other ingredients, but fruits, raisins and candied peel. Then there was the deep yellow layer of almond icing and above that the white icing, with maybe a silver ball or the shred of an initial where it had been cut off on someone's name or a greeting. The flavour was exotic but that was secondary. One slept with it under one's pillow in the hope that the initials of one's own future spouse would be delivered up in a dream. If it did not happen that night then some other night, in a year or two or three, when another piece of wedding cake hopefully would arrive in the post. I was vexed with my mother for suggesting him, even as a joke. I felt defiled.

When I came to go away to boarding school Jack gave me a present wrapped in several sheets of damp newspaper. It was a blue propelling pencil whose lead was so weak that at first usage it broke. Later I gave it to a nun who was collecting for the black babies. Within a week he wrote to me and since our letters were censored the nun asked who this gentleman was.

'My uncle, Sister,' I said and was surprised that I could lie with such facility. It was almost dark but as it was not the appointed time to put on the lights, we were obliged to read our letters in the half light. I went over to the window and pushed aside a castor oil plant and read his effusion.

I hope you are well and attending diligently to your studies. I shall be curious to learn if geometry is your pet subject as it was mine; three cheers for Pythagoras! Your Mam and Dad are fine, we converse as usual on world affairs, and we miss your bright pertinent contributions.

My wine shop is flourishing, a gentleman travelled from the North of Ireland last week to sample, and later to purchase, a particular vintage of mine. It was my very own, concocted from the offerings of the ditches, rhubarb, elderberry and parsnip mixed to give a subtle bouquet.

(I knew that if anyone made the wine it was the maternity nurse.)

I am still writing poems and brushing up on Swift and Goldsmith, indeed have dialogues with them when I peruse the highways and the byways. The name of Holland will one day be illustrious; if not for one thing, then for another. The weather is clement, though there was a downpour yesterday and I was obliged to take precautions.

(I could see him putting basins in the passage and dish cloths on the shop floor to catch some of the rain as it poured through the leaking roof.)

Here is a little surprise with which to supplement your budget. Do not allow the good nuns to twist your head in a fervent direction, and remember your promise to your friend,
                                                         JACK

He had enclosed a money order for five shillings and I could hardly believe it. Its white crinkled paper with the heavy black lettering assured me that he had indeed sent this amount but I could not know why.

It was a clear starry night when I came home for my Christmas holidays as I got off the bus and walked up the field.

It was a pleasure to feel the darkness again, to smell the wet grass and the rotting toadstools. The dogs jumped on me, licked my face and were hysterical with welcome. Inside the door Mama stood waiting to embrace me, and beside her was Jack. He grinned foolishly at me and hurt the two fingers next to my ringed finger by giving me an iron handshake. My new friend, Lydia, had loaned me her signet ring, so that I would think of her constantly.

Mama had a table laid in the breakfast room, and there were sausage rolls, mince pies and iced orange cake. The turf fire sent up rainbow-coloured flames and to smell it again after so many months made me realise how cold and unnatural was our life in the convent.

'Yours truly is a bit of an antiquarian now,' Jack said to me across the table.

'Oh,' was all I could say in reply.

'Yes, when searching for mushrooms last harvest I found a brooch which proved to be unique. But keep this under your hat, because of course a lot of hooligans would endeavour to imitate me. It's bronze. I've interested some authorities from Dublin and they are travelling to see it early in the New Year.'

Mama winked at me. 'Will you carry a candle upstairs, till we get a pillow that I want to air for you.'

We linked as we climbed the stairs, and for once she did not warn me about spilling grease on the old turkey carpet. Anyhow we would melt it next day onto a piece of brown paper either with a hot iron or a hot knife. I wanted to sit on the landing step and discuss everything, how my hair once got nits in it, and the disgrace that the nun had made of me, then ask if Dada had been drinking, and if the harvest had been good and therefore would we be able to pay my fees. When I shone the candle on her face Mama was laughing.

'It's Jack,' she said, 'he imagines things now. He's not all there. He digs in the Protestant graveyard every night and finds nothing only old bottles and chamber pots and broken glass domes.'

'Has he any friends?' I asked.

'Only us . . .' she said.

Jack beamed at me when I came downstairs and a little later when he was leaving it was inside the neck of my jumper and not Mama's that he dropped two toffees. I was only back a month in the convent when Mama wrote to tell me that Jack was building a large two-storey house, three miles outside the village. She also said that there was a rumour he was getting married to a girl from Longford and that the maternity nurse got shingles when she heard it. He was then probably sixty. There was no telling how he made contact with this lady in Longford unless it was by post, but it was said that such a lady existed, and that her name was Cissy. Most afternoons he shut shop and went to build without any help at all, not even a handyman or a plasterer. As a consequence the house took three years and my mother wrote to tell me what it was like. 'Jack's house is at last complete. Your father and I were brought to see it last Sunday. "Terrible" is the only word I could use. The roof is not slated, the window frames very crooked and the exterior a bilious yellow colour which he called ochre. The road up to it is a swamp. Of course Jack thinks it is marvellous and he has called it "Sweet Auburn" no less. He is dying to show it to you.'

When I came home on a summer holiday having finished with the convent, I aspired towards Dublin and resented having to stay at home and listen to depressing conversations. I was sarcastic to my mother, shunned my father and spent most of the time upstairs fitting on clothes, my own clothes and my mother's clothes. A youngster came from the village to say that Jack wanted to see me at three o'clock. My mother said that she felt it was propitious. I had done well in my examination and she believed that Jack was going to give me ten or twenty pounds. I hoped she was right as I yearned for the money to buy style. He was waiting for me outside the shop, sitting on the window sill with an oilskin thrown over one shoulder in jaunty toreador fashion. He looked happy and he waved to me from fifty yards away.

'What a picture,' he said as he stood up and with a nod indicated that we weren't going to sit there in view of the village. The blind was down in his shop and I asked if it was the half day.

'No, but yours truly is his own boss,' he said and took great strides up the hill and passed the chapel and the graveyard.

'Where are we going?' I asked.

'To my country abode,' he said.

It began to rain, the drops came singly at first and then with a great urgency and he used this as an excuse for chivalry, and placed the oilskin over my shoulders. We walked out that road and then up the track to the damp spectacle of a solitary house. He was impatient to get to it. There being no gate he lifted a strand of the rusty barbed wire and helped me in, into the rectangular patch which enclosed the house and where the nettles flourished. The house looked haunted and the windows were dirty. A rat slunk deftly through a hole under the privet hedge and if Jack saw it he certainly made no reference to it. Birds flew wildly in and out of the eaves and chattered as if they were angry with us, as if their occupancy of the place was challenged by our visit. In the field beyond the barbed wire was a very small old donkey whose hairs had come off in patches and who stared at us but did not bray. Jack muttered something about having flower beds made later on and added that he was also partial to an arch over which roses could tumble in June. It was June and all that blossomed was the ragwort and the masses of buttercups, both yellow, both bright.

As we stood there he was pointing to certain features of the house, the fanlight above the hall door which he described as neo-Georgian and the door itself which was made of deal. For all his talk its features were very prosaic and very wanting. It was a square two-storey house, its front pebble-dashed and painted over this dark muddy yellow. The curtainless windows were like long mourners looking out onto the neglected garden. Its only feature, if one can call it that, was that it was on an incline and there was a fine view of ploughed land and meadow leading to the road. I went to look through one of the long windows but he intercepted me. The tour had to be done properly and with him as guide. Impatience seized me and I looked anyhow and in the drawing room saw the bare boards spattered with paint and in the middle of the floor, incongruously, a marble fireplace. Carrara marble, as he said. It was a sign of the grandeur that he aspired to. He conceded that the house needed a bit more work and then declared that what it surely needed was the woman's touch, that seemly eye that would know where to hang a mirror, or where to put a little whatnot and which portrait to place over the fireplace so that visitors would sit there with a sense of enrichment. I listened to his ramblings, resenting the fact that the high wet grass was harming my new sandals and draining the beige dye out of them. Did we, I wondered, ever pay him back the money he had given the Bailiff. He was probably paid in kind and hunks of cake and bacon and even an embroidered tablecloth would have to suffice for much of the money. I did not care. Only one thing was uppermost in me and it was flight, and in my fancies I had no idea that no matter how distant the flight or how high I soared those people were entangled in me.

I had to say something so I said 'It's very secluded.'

'Not when there's two of us . . .' he said.

He went round to the side to fetch the key which was kept in a can. I felt chilled by the sight of it all – nettles, thistles, ragwort and such an emanation of damp from the house itself that it seemed more dismal than any outhouse. Coming back twirling the big key he winked at me slyly and then it had happened before I had time to repel him. Jack had turned the key in the door, then he turned, lifted me up in his arms and carried me over the threshold, triumphantly shouting 'Hallelujah . . . ours, ours, ours.' He said for long he had envisaged such a scene and only wished he had brought a ring. His mouth and nose were lowered towards my face and I saw him as a great vampire about to demand a kiss. I struggled out of his arms and ran towards the barbed wire accusing him of being a horrible man. Either he was too shocked or too ashamed to follow but

I need not have gone at such a helter-skelter down the dirt track, because as I looked back I saw that he was standing as stationary and as forlorn as a poplar tree. He did not move or beckon.

Jack stopped visiting our house, crossed the road when he saw my mother and avoided my father after Mass. It was then the maternity nurse became essential. Now that we were banished she made him soda bread and when she delivered it she collected dirty socks from the table or from a chair where they were slung. She darned them and even began to talk of plans for the unused parlour, she fancied an oil stove to be put in there. Since the girl from Longford had not materialised everyone thought that he would marry the maternity nurse and indeed so did she. But after six months of washing and baking and even repairing the lace curtains on the upstairs landing she asked the Parish Priest to have a word with Jack. The Priest called one Sunday evening and since the public house was shut the front door was ceremoniously lifted back. It had swollen in the rain. Jack threw a newspaper over a kitchen chair and asked His Reverence to sit down and to please forgive the humility of the place, and to have a drop of sherry, or better still a glass of malt.

'Well now Jack, there's none of us getting younger, and time is passing, and you are keeping company with a very nice lady and isn't it time that you thought of settling down.'

Those were the very words the Parish Priest used because he described the incident in detail to my mother, the day she had Mass said in our house.

'Marriage, Father,' said Jack, 'is out of the question. I was betrothed for a long number of years to a certain little lady in this parish, who jilted me. It has embittered my ideals about the opposite sex, it has cauterised me from ever entering on another alliance, indeed it has ruined my life.'

Jack was soon without the ministerings of the maternity nurse, and in time he became more remote and did not even talk to his customers. He just served them the drink and watched while they drank and brooded. He lost interest in his two-storey house and one evening some children who were picking mushrooms saw flames in the front window and hurried to look inside, thinking it had caught fire. Inside a group of tinkers squatted on the floor, eating and drinking, and they had made a big fire in the grate. When told of this Jack said he would get the Sergeant to deal with it but whenever the tinkers came, they did not sleep out in the fields as before but used the shelter of the house.

The following winter he got shingles and used to open his shop at odd hours, when it suited him. As I got older, I thought of him, of how embarrassed he must have been and how callous I must have seemed. I wanted to talk to him and somehow to make amends. My mother warned me that he was very peculiar and that if I went to the shop he would not let me past the door but would drive me out as he had done to her. I said that I would follow him from Mass. I sat through the coughing and the croaking, inhaling the damp smell of tweed coats, looking at all the faces that I had almost forgotten, faces worn and twisted like the trees. He was bald, stooped and he prayed feverishly on his black horn rosary beads. His fingers could have been an old woman's so small were they, so gnarled. The chapel itself seemed a smaller and humbler place and I thought of the missionaries and the terror of their sermons. The Parish Priest was very slow and at times hesitated as if he had forgotten the words. At the last Gospel, Jack jumped up and left. Forewarned about this I too got up, genuflected and left. He hurried out under the cypress trees and opened the church gate but did not wait to close it. It clanged.

'Jack, Jack.' I could not shout lest it be disrespectful to the proceedings in the church. I closed the gate and walked quickly, all the while calling, but he pretended not to hear. He took great strides and it was clear that he was avoiding me. I caught up with him as he reached his own shop door and was pushing it in.

'Jack, it's lovely to see you.'

He heard but did not turn. He went in, pushed the door shut and immediately drew a bolt. I stood there thinking that he would change his mind. The grey gauze blind that had once had the name 'Vintner' printed on it was like filament. Any minute it seemed as if it might disintegrate. I tapped and tapped but he did not relent. Indeed I did not know if he stood there, vacillating, or if he had gone on tiptoe into the kitchen and was brewing a cup of tea. Walking down the road his sadness and hidden ways contrasted terribly with the bright bells of the fuchsia and the sounds of motorists hooting happily as they went home from Mass. His gloom had cut him off and his friends would not rally until they came as mourners.

When he died he left his premises to a cousin whom we had never seen and scarcely knew of. Realising that he had not remembered us at all, in his Will, and reciting the motto about 'blood being thicker than water', my mother said that she was genuinely surprised that he hadn't left her a decanter or a biscuit barrel. But I think her disappointment was not so much to do with graft as it was deference to romance, which although she stoutly denounced, in some part of her mysterious being she cherished it and all her life believed that it would come her way.

Savages

Mabel's family lived in a cottage at the end of our avenue and we were forever going back and forth, helping, borrowing tea or sugar or the paper, or linament, agog for each other's news. We knew of Mabel's homecoming for weeks, but what we did not know was whether she would come by bus or car, and whether she would arrive in daylight or dusk. She was coming from Australia, making most of the journey by ship, and then crossing on the sail boat to Dublin, and then by train to our station that was indeed rustic and where a passenger seldom got off. She would be tired. She would be excited. She would be full of strange stories and strange impressions. How long would she stay? What would she look like? Would her hair be permed? What presents, or what knick knacks would she bring? Would she have an accent? Oh what novelty. These and a thousand other questions assailed us and as the time got nearer her name and her arrival was on everyone's lips. I was allowed to help her mother on the Saturday and in my eagerness I set out at cock-crow having brought six fresh eggs and the loan of our egg beater. First task was to clear out the upstairs room. It smelt musty. Mice scrambled there because her family kept their oats in it. It was an attic room with a skylight window and a slanting ceiling. In fact it was only half a room because of the way one kept bumping one's head on the low distempered ceiling. My job was to scoop oats with a trowel and pour it into a sack. So buoyed up was I with anticipation that now and then I became absent-minded and the oats slid out of the sack once again. From time to time her mother would say 'I hope she hasn't an accident', or 'I hope she hasn't broke her pledge', but these things were said to disguise or temper her joy. The thing is

Mabel's coming had brought hope and renewal into her life.

Mabel had been gone for ten years and the only communications in between had been her monthly letter and some photographs. The photos were very dim and they were always with other girls, smirking, so that one didn't see what she was like in repose. Also she always wore a hat so that her features were disguised. Mabel worked as a lady's companion and her letters told of this lady, her wrath, the sunflowers in her garden and the beauty of her German piano that was made of cherry wood.

'I expect she'll stay for the summer,' her mother said, and I thought that a bit optimistic. Who would want to stay three or four months in our Godforsaken townland. Nothing happened except the land was ploughed, the crops were put down, there was a harvest, a threshing, then geese were sent to feast on the stubble and soon the land was bare again. None of the women wore cosmetics and in the local chemist shop the jars of cold cream and vanishing cream used to go dry because of no demand. Of course we read about fashions in a magazine and we knew, my sisters and I knew, that ladies wore tweed costumes the colour of mulberries, and that they sometimes had silk handkerchiefs steeped in perfume which they wore underneath their bodices for effect. Not for a second did I think Mabel would stay long but had I said anything her mother would have sent me home. We carried a trestle bed up, put the clean sheets on and the blankets and then hung a ribbon of adhesive paper for the flies to stick to. The place still smelt musty but her mother said that was to be expected and that if Mabel was ashamed of her origins, she had another guess coming.

We went downstairs to get on with the baking. Her mother cracked the six fresh eggs into the bowl and beat them to a frothlike consistency. Then she got out the halves of orange peel and lemon peel and in the valleys were crusts of sugar that were like ice. I longed for a piece. I was put sieving the flour and I did it so energetically that the flour swirled in the air, making the atmosphere snow-white. At that moment her husband came in and demanded his dinner. She said couldn't he see she was making a cake. She referred him to the little meat safe that was attached to a tree outside in the garden whereupon he growled and wielded his ash plant. It seems there was nothing in the meat safe, only buttermilk.

'Don't addle me,' she said.

'Is it grass you would have me eat,' he said and I saw that he was in imminent danger of picking up the whisked eggs and pitching them out in the yard where we would never be able to retrieve them because hens, ducks and pigs paddled in the muck out there.

'Can't you give me a chance,' she said but seeing that he was about to explode, she stooped, avoiding a possible blow, and then from under a dish she hauled out an ox tongue that she had boiled that morning. It was of course meant for Mabel but she realised that she had better be expedient. As she cut the tongue he watched, barely containing his rage. As I saw her put the knife to it I thought poor oxen had not much of a life either living or dead. She cut it thinly as she was trying to economise. In the silence we heard a mouse as it got caught in the trap that we had just put down in Mabel's room. Its screech was both sudden and beseeching. Her husband picked up a slice of the tongue with his hand, being too impatient to wait for it to be handed on the plate. I too wanted to taste it but not by itself. I would have loved it with a piece of pickle so that the taste was not like oxen but like something artificial, something out of a jar. He ate by the fire munching loudly, and asking me for another cut of bread, and quick. He drank his tea from an enamel mug and I could hear it going glug-glug down his gullet. He had never addressed a civil word to me in his life.

The baked cake was the most beautiful sight. It was dark gold in colour, it had risen beautifully and there were small cracks on the top into which she secretly poured a drop of whiskey to give it, as she said, an aroma. I asked if she was going to ice it but she seemed to resent that question. For some absurd reason I began to wonder who Mabel would marry, because of course she was not yet married and she must not be left on the shelf as that was a most mortifying role.

'You can go home now,' her mother said to me.

I looked at her. If looks can talk then these should have. My look was an invocation. It was saying 'Let me come for Mabel's arrival.' I lingered thinking that she would say it but she didn't. I praised the cake. I was lavish in my praise of it, of the clean windows, the floor polish, the three mice caught and consigned to the fire, of everything. It was all in vain. She did not invite me.

The next day was agony. Would I be let go? It was still not broached and I tried a thousand ruses and just as many imprecations. I would pick up the clock that was lying face down, and if I had guessed the time to within minutes then I would surely go. A butterfly had got caught between the two panes of opened window and I thought if it finds its way out unaided, then I shall go. In there it struggled and beat its wings, it kept going around in circles to no purpose, yet miraculously shot up and sailed out into the air, a vision of soft fluttering orange-brown. Not to go would be torture. But worse than that would be if my sisters were let go and I was told to mind the house. It sometimes happened. Why mind a house that was solid and vaster than oneself. Extreme diligence took possession of me and such a spurt of tidiness that my mother said it was to our house Mabel should be arriving. If only that were so!

After the tea, when I had washed up the dishes, I could no longer contain myself and I began to snivel. My mother pretended not to notice. She was changing her clothes in the kitchen. She often changed there and held the good clothes in front of the fire to air them. The rooms upstairs were damp, the wardrobes were damp and when you put on your good clothes you could feel the damp seeping in to your bones. She was brusque. She said why ringlets and why one's best cardigan. I cried more. She said to put it out of one's head and announced that none of the children were going as the McCann kitchen was far too small for hordes. She said to cut out the sobs and do one's homework instead. While my father shaved I went under the table to pray. It was evident he was in a bad mood because of the way he scraped the stubble off his chin. He said that not even a day like this could be enjoyed. He said why did he have to fodder cattle and my mother said because there was no one else to do it.

After they had gone my sisters and I decided to make pancakes. As it happened my elder sister nearly set fire to the house because of the amount of paraffin she threw on to the stove. I shall never forget it. It was like the last day with flames rising out of the stove, panels of orange flame going up the walls and my other sister and I screaming at her to quench it, quench it. The first thing to hand was a can of milk which we threw on it in terror. Luckily we conquered it and all that remained was a smell of paraffin and a terrible smell of burnt milk. The pancake project was abandoned and we spent the next hour trying to air the place and clean the stove. Docility had certainly taken hold of us by the time my mother and father returned. It was dark and we could hear the hasp of the gate and then the dogs bounding towards the door and then the latch lifting. My mother was first. She always came first so as to be able to put on the kettle for him and so as to get on with her tasks. First thing we noticed was the parcel under her arm. It was in tissue paper and it had been opened at one end. My sister grabbed it as my mother wrinkled up her nose and said was there something burning. We denied that and harried her to tell, tell. Mabel had come, was tired from her journey, spoke in a funny accent and said that in Australia wattles meant mimosa trees and not mere sticks or stones.

By then my father had arrived and said that he was a better-looking man than Mabel himself and then did an impersonation of her accent. It was like no accent I had ever heard. My father said that the only interesting thing about her was that she backed horses and had been to race meetings in Sydney. My mother said that she had been marooned out on some sheep station and had met very few people only the shearers and the lady she worked for. My mother pronounced on her as being haggard and with a skin tough and wizened from the heat. The present turned out to be pale-blue silk pyjamas. I could see my mother's reaction – immense disappointment that was bordering on disgust. She had hoped for a dress or a blouse, she had certainly hoped for a wearable. For another thing pyjamas were shameful, sinful. Men wore pyjamas, women wore nightgowns. Shame and disgrace. My mother folded them up quickly so as not to let my father see them, in case it gave him ideas. She bundled them into a press and it was plain to see that she was nettled. She would have even liked a remnant so as to be able to make dresses for us. It seemed that the homecoming was something of an anti-climax and that even Mabel's father couldn't understand a word that she had said. It seems that the men who had come to vet her agreed that she wasn't worth tuppence and the women were most disappointed by her attire. They had expected her to be wearing high-heeled court shoes, preferably suede, and it seems she was wearing leather shoes that were almost, but not quite, flat. To make matters worse they were tan and her stockings were tan and her skin was slightly tan and along with all that she was in a bright red suit. My mother said she looked like a scarecrow and was very loud.

Next day it rained. The rain beat against the window and every so often the hailstones pelted it. The sky was ink-black and even when a cloud broke the silver inside was dark and oppressive presaging a storm. I was sent around the house to close the windows and put cloths on the sills in case the rain soaked through. I saw a figure coming up the avenue and thought it might be a begging woman with a coat over her head. When we heard the knocking on the back door my mother opened it sharply, poised as she was for hostilities.

'Mabel,' my mother said, surprised, and I ran to see her. She was a small woman with black bobbed hair, a very long nose and eyes which were grey and darting. She wore rubber overshoes which she began to remove and as she held on to the side of the sink I stood in front of her. She asked me was I me and said that the last time she had seen me I was screaming my head off in a hammock, in the garden. Somehow she expected me to be pleased by this news or at least to be amused.

What struck me most about her was her abruptness. In no time she was complaining about those two old fogies, her mother and father, and telling us that she was not going to sit by a fire with them all day long and discuss rheumatism. Also she complained about the house, said it wasn't big enough.

My mother calmed her with tea and cake and my father asked her what kind of horses they bred in Australia. He wagered a bet that they were not as thoroughbred as the Irish horses. To that my mother gave a grunt since our horses brought us nothing but disappointment and debt. When pressed for other news Mabel said that she had seen a thing or two, her eyes had been opened, but she would not say in what way. She hinted at having undergone some terrible shock and I thought that possibly she had been jilted. She described a tea they drank out of glasses, sitting on the verandah at sun-down. My mother said it was a wonder the hot tea didn't crack the glasses. Mabel said she should never have come home and that when she wakened up that morning and heard the rain on the skylight she had yearned to go back. Yet in no time she was contradicting herself and said it was all 'outback' in Australia and who wanted to live in an outback. My father said he'd make a match for her and gradually she cheered up as she sat at the side of the stove and from time to time popped one or other foot in the lower oven for warmth. Her stockings were lisle and a very unfortunate colour, rather like the colour of the stirabout that we gave to the hens and the chickens. She had an accent at certain moments but she lost it whenever she talked about her own people. She said their house was nothing but a cabin, a thatched cabin. When she said indiscreet things she laughed and persisted until she got someone to join in.

'Mabel, you're a scream,' my mother said while also pretending to be shocked at the indiscretions.

Very reluctantly my father had gone out to fodder and Mabel was drinking blackberry wine from a beautiful stemmed glass. When she held the glass up, colours danced on her cheek and then ran down her throat just as the wine was running down inside. Presently her face got flushed, and her eyes teary and she confessed that she had thought of Ireland night and day for the ten years, had saved to come home and now realised that she had made a frightful mistake. She sniffled and then took out a spotted handkerchief.

'Faraway hills look green,' my mother said, and the two of them sighed as if a wealth of meaning had been exchanged. My mother proposed a few visits they could make on Sundays and buoyed up by the wine and these promises Mabel said that she had a second present for my mother but that in the commotion the previous evening she was unable to find it. She said it must be somewhere in the bottom of her trunk. It was to be a brush and comb set, with matching bone tray. We never saw it.

It took several months before Mabel paid me any attention. She had favoured my sisters because they were older and because they had ideas about how to set hair, how to paint toenails and how to use an emery board or a nail buffer. It was either of them she took on her Sunday excursion, and it was either of them she summoned on the way home from school so as to sit with her in the garden and chat. It proved to be a scorching summer and Mabel had put two deckchairs in their front garden and had planted lupins. She never let anyone pass without hollering as she was avid for company. In the autumn my sisters went away to school and suddenly Mabel was in need of a walking companion. My mother had long since ceased to go with her, because Mabel was mad for gallivanting, and had worn out her welcome in every house up the town, and in many houses up the country.

One Sunday she chose me. It was the very same as if she had just arrived home because to me she was still a mysterious stranger. We were calling on a family who lived in the White House. It had been given that name because the money for it had come from relatives in America. It was a yellow, two-storey, pebble-dash house set in its own grounds with a heart-shaped lawn in front. At the edge of the lawn there was a flower bed in which there had been dark red tulips, and at the far end was a little house with an electricity plant. They were the only people in the neighbourhood to have electricity, and that plus the tulips, plus the candlewick bedspreads, plus the legacies from America, made theirs the most enticing house in the county. As we went up their drive my white canvas shoes adhered to the tarmac which was fresh and melting. The house with its lace-edged fawn blinds was quiet and suggested luxury and harmony. Needless to say they had cross dogs and at the first sound of a yelp Mabel lagged behind, while telling me to stand my ground and not give off an adrenalin smell. A boy who was clipping the privet hedge saved us by calling the dogs and holding them by their tawny manes. They snarled like lions.

Since we were not expected a certain coolness ensued. The mistress of the house was lying down, her husband was in bed sick, and the little serving girl Annie didn't ask us to cross the threshold. All of a sudden the dummies appeared. They were brother and sister and though I had often heard of them, and even seen them at Mass, devoutly fingering their rosary beads I had no idea that they would be so effusive. They descended on us. They mauled us. They strove with tongue and lips and every other feature to talk to us, to communicate. The movements of their hands were fluent and wizard. They pulled us into the kitchen where the female dummy put me up on a chair so she could look at the pleats in my coat, and then the buttons. She herself was dressed in a terrible hempen dress that was almost to her ankles. Her brother was in an ill-fitting coarse suit. They were in-laws of the mistress of the house and it was rumoured that she did not like them. She was trying to say something urgent when the mistress who had risen from her nap came in and greeted us somewhat reservedly. Soon we were seated around the kitchen table and while Mabel and the mistress discussed who had been at Mass, and who had taken Holy Communion, and who had new style, the dummies were pestering me and trying to get me to go outside. They would puff their cheeks out in an encouragement to make me puff mine.

Mabel and the mistress of the house began to talk about her husband. They moved closer together. They were like two people conspiring. A terrible word was said. I heard it. It was the word haemorrhage. He was haemorrhaging. Only women did that. I began to go dizzy with dread. I gripped the chair by its sides then put one hand on the table for further security, and began to hum. My face must have been blazing because soon the dummies realised there was something wrong and thinking only one thing they pulled me towards a door and down a passage to a lavatory. It was a cold spot and there was a cannister of scouring powder left on a ledge, as if Annie had been cleaning and had gone off in a hurry or a sulk. They kept knocking on the door and when I came out inspected me carefully to see that my coat was pulled down. The lady dummy whose pet name was Babs drew me into the kitchen and as we stood in front of the fire she did a little caper. She had a tea cloth in one hand and held it out as if she was keeping a bull at bay. She was told by the mistress of the house to put it down or she would be sent to the dairy. Her twin brother affected the most terrible huff by letting out moans that were nearly animal, and moving his eyes hither and thither and at such a speed I thought they would drop out. He too was threatened with a sojourn in the dairy. At length so chastised were they that they each took a chair and sat with their backs to us and refused when asked to turn around.

The mistress said they needed a good smacking.

After an age the mistress offered us a tour of the house. When she opened the drawing-room door what one first saw was the sun streaming in through the long panes of glass and bouncing on the polished furniture. She muttered something about having forgotten to draw the blinds. Pictures of cows and ripening corn hung on either side of the marble mantelpiece, and in the tiled fireplace there was an arrangement of artificial flowers, tea roses, yellow, apricot and gold. Not only that, but the flowers in a round thick rug matched. To look at it you felt certain that no one had stepped on that rug, that it was pristine like a wall-hanging. Its pile and its softness made one long to kneel or bask in it. Mabel of course commented on the various things, on the curtains for instance that were sumptuous, on the pelmet that matched, on the long plaited cord by which the curtains could be folded or parted. Pulling it I had a fancy that I was opening the curtains of a theatre and that presently through the window would come a troupe of performers. The mistress of the house was pleased at our excitedness and as a reward she took something from the china cabinet and let me hold it. It was a miniature cabin made of black-thorn wood. It had a tiny door that opened the merest chink.

Next we saw the breakfast room and then the dining room which by contrast was dark and sombre, save for the gleam of the silver salver on the sideboard. Next we saw the bathroom with its green bath, matching basin and candlewick bathmat. But we were not brought up the last flight of stairs which led to the bedrooms, lest our footsteps waken her husband and make him want to get up. He was craving to get up and go out in the fields. Up there, the darkness was extreme because of a stained-glass window. The hallway seemed a bit sepulchral and quite different from the downstairs room. I could hear the crows cawing ceaselessly and it occurred to me that before long there would be a death in the house, as I believe it occurred to them, because they looked at one another, and shook their heads in silent commiseration.

The kitchen clock chimed five and still we sat in hope of something to eat. Mabel rubbed her stomach to indicate that she was hungry while the mistress put on her apron and said that soon it would be milking time and time to feed calves and do a million things. Half-heartedly she offered us a cup of tea. There was nothing festive about it, it was just a cup of tea off a tray, four scones and a slab of strong-smelling yellow country butter. It was not fashioned into little burr balls as I had expected. Mabel kicked me under the table, knowing my disappointment. There was no cake and no cold meat. Mabel judged people's hospitality by whether they gave her cold meat or not.

On the way home she lamented that there was not a bit of

lamb, no chicken, no beetroot or freshly made potato salad with scallions.

It was a warm evening and the ripe corn in the fields was a sight to behold. Here and there it had lodged but for the most part it was high and victorious, ready for the thresher. She said, 'I wonder what they're doing in Australia now', and ventured to say that they missed her. She asked did I like those flowers my mother fashioned by putting twirls of silver and gold paper over the ears of corn. When I said no, she hurrahed. It meant that she and I were now friends, allies. Of course I knew that I had betrayed my mother and would pay for it either by being punished or by having bouts of remorse. She took out her flapjack to apply some powder. It was a tiny gold flapjack and the powder puff was in shreds.

Mabel made a face at herself and then asked if I had a boy yet. The word boy like the word haemorrhage threatened to make me faint. She said soon I would have a boy and to be careful not to let him lay a finger on me because it was a well-known fact that one could get a craze for it, and end up ruined, imprisoned in the Magdalen Laundry, until you had a baby. She might have launched into more graphic tales but that a car came around the corner and she jumped up and waved so as to summon a lift.

In the town we called on a woman to whom Mabel had given a crocheted tea cosy and our reward was two long glasses of lemonade, and a plate of currant-topped biscuits. Mabel was prodigal with her promises. She volunteered to crochet a bed-cover and asked the women if there were any favourite colours or more important if there were any colours she could not abide. She burped as we walked down the hill and over the bridge towards home. It was getting dark and the birds were busy with both song and chatter. Every bird in every tree had something to say. As we passed the houses we could hear people banging buckets and dishes and by the light of a lantern we saw one woman feeding calves at her doorstep. As each calf finished its quota its head was pulled out to give the next calf a chance. Those whose heads were outside the bucket kept butting and kicking and were in no way satisfied. We knew the woman but we did not linger as Mabel whispered that it would be dull old blather about new milk and sucking calves. Mabel did not like the country and had no interest in tillage, sunsets or landscape. She objected to pools of water in the roadside, pools of water in the meadows, the corncrake in the evening and the cocks crowing at dawn. As we walked along she took my hand and said that henceforth I was to be her walking companion. It was a thrill to feel her gloved hand awkwardly pressing on mine. Untold adventures lay ahead.

Sometimes on our travels we met with a shut door or we were not asked to cross the threshold. But these rebuffs meant nothing to her and she merely designated the people as being ignorant and countrified. As luck would have it, our third Sunday we struck on a most welcoming house. It was a remote house, first along a tarred road then a dirt road and then across a stream. Our hosts were two young girls who were home from England and great was their pleasure in receiving company. They were home for a month but were already aching to go back. The older one, Betty, was a nurse and Moira her sister was a buyer in a shop and consequently they dressed like fashion plates. We went every Sunday knowing that they would be waiting for us and they had got their father and mother out of the house visiting cousins. It was such a thrill as we got to the stream and took off our shoes and stockings, then let out raucous sounds about the temperature of the water, but really to alert them. It was a clean silvery water with stones beneath, some round and smooth, some pointed. They would hear us and run down the slope to welcome us while also asking in exaggerated accents if the water was like ice. To hear our names called was the zenith of welcome.

We would be brought through the kitchen into the parlour while they told Nora, their younger sister, to put the kettle on and to be smart about it. The parlour was dark, with red embossed wallpaper, and we all sat very upright, on hard horsehair sofas. It so happened that I had begun to do impersonations of the dummies and immediately they requested it. As a reward I was given a slice of coconut cake that they had brought back from England, and that was kept in a tin with a harlequin figure on the lid. It was a bit dry but much more exotic than their homemade cake. Mabel would let her tongue roll over her top and bottom teeth, then ask was there any meat left, whereupon Moira would lift a plate that exactly adhered to another plate and reveal that she had kept Mabel a lunch.

'You sport, you,' Mabel said. Her accent would suddenly sound Australian.

'Don't mention it,' Moira would say airily.

Our visits sustained them. With us they could discuss fashion and fit on their finery, then later do the Lambeth Walk in the big flagged kitchen. Doing this led to howls of laughter. Always, one of us got the step wrong and the whole thing had to be recommenced. Even their sheepdog thought it was hilarious and moved about in a clumsy way to the strains of the music from the crackling wind-up gramophone. We alternated at being ladies or gents and we had conversations that ladies and gents have.

'Do you come here often?' or 'Next dance please' or 'Care for a mineral?' was what our partners said. Afterwards we lounged in the chairs breathless, and then we set out for a walk, or as they called it, 'a ramble'. It was on one of these rambles that we met Matt. An auspicious meeting it proved to be. He had the reputation of being a queer fellow, a recluse. He had gone to Canada, made some money and had come back to marry his childhood sweetheart, but was jilted on the eve of the wedding. Some said that the marriage was broken off because the two families couldn't agree about land, others said she thought his manners too gruff, and at any rate she fled to England. Matt was a tall man with a thin face, a wart and longish hair. He looked educated as if he spent time poring over books and almanacs. It seems he had new-fangled ideas about planting trees whereas most of the farmers just felled them for firewood. There was something original about him. It may have been his gravity or his silence. He could go into a public house and drink a pint of porter without passing a word to anyone, even the publican. He never visited any of his neighbours and had his Christmas dinner at home, with his brother who was supposed to be a bit missing in the head. Matt met us down by the river. He had a stick in his hand and his hat was pushed back on his head. He must have been driving cattle because he was perspiring a bit, but he still looked dignified. Moira had picked some sorrel and was eating it saying it was like lemon juice, and very good for one's skin. He stood apart from us but at the same time he was taking stock. At least that's what one read from his smile. There was mockery in his smile but there was also scrutiny. Betty and Moira knew him, knew his moods and pretended not to notice that he was there.

'Wouldn't you all fancy sugar plums,' he said to no one in particular. Mabel was the first to respond.

'Are they ripe?' she asked.

'They're ripe,' he said but in such an insolent way we were not sure if he was telling the truth or just tantalising us.

'I much prefer damsons,' Moira said.

'Damsons are too tart,' Mabel said, 'damsons are only fit for jam.'

'Please yourselves,' he said and sauntered off letting a whistle escape from his lips. Mabel called out were we invited or not.

'As you wish,' he said, and nodding to each other we followed. I thought we were like cows ambling across a field, not quite a herd, and not herded but all heading in the same direction and feeling aimless. It was a beautiful autumn evening with the sun a vivid flame and in the sky around it rivers of red and pink and washed gold. His was a two-storey stone house and the front door was closed. It looked very dead and secretive. There was a hand pump in the yard and as he passed it, he worked the handle a few times to replenish the trough underneath. We could hear the calves lowing and suddenly the cock started to crow as if disapproving. Hens ran in all directions and there were two small bonhams wallowing in some mud. It was anything but cheerful. He did not invite us in.

In contrast the orchard was a great tangle of trees and fruit bushes all smothered in convolvulus and the grass needed to be scythed. The apples looked so tempting, blood-red and polished while the plums were like dusky globes ready to drop off. He put one to his lips. It was the first time that anything approaching pleasure touched his countenance.

'Help yourselves,' he said, and I thought perhaps he is a generous man, perhaps he is kind inside and only needs four or five girls giggling and gorging to draw him out. Mabel was intrepid as she picked three plums and debated which to sample first. The two girls, having been to England, were much more polite and did not rhapsodise over the taste and did not drip juice on to their chins. Mabel declared that there would be no stopping her now, that she would come Sunday after Sunday while the fruits lasted. He picked up a lid of a tin can that had been lying in the grass, lined it with a few wide leaves and handed it to me, with the instruction that we were to bring some home. It was obvious that he took great pleasure in the fact that we were so excited.

'No one ever eats them ... they just rot,' he said.

'That's a shame,' Mabel said and she winked at him, and he winked back. It is an odd thing how a face can suddenly alter. It was not that she appeared beautiful but she had a kind of lustre and her glances were knowing and piquant.

'Every autumn,' she said and I thought of life as being charmed, a series of autumns just like then, the sun going down, the beautiful globes of fruit, like lamps waiting to be plucked, our happiness undimmed. In my hand I felt the softness of a plum, yet knew the hardness of the stone deep within it and I knew that my optimism was unwise.

'How long are you home for?' he asked Moira.

'Long enough,' she said and shrugged. Her reply both shocked and dazzled me. I thought what a wonderful way to talk to a man, to be at once polite and distant, to be scornful without being downright rude. Then he broached the subject of the carnival. The carnival was to take place at the end of the month. Mabel asked if he'd take her for a ride on the swingboats or the bumper cars and he smiled at each one of us and said he hoped he would have the pleasure.

'We'll be gone back,' Betty said.

'You ought to stay for the carnival,' Mabel said but I knew that she did not mean it and was looking forward to a time when she would see Matt without the competition of two younger, comelier girls. God knows what fancies were stirred in her then. Perhaps she thought – a bachelor, a two-storey house, a man she could cook for, prosperity, a wedding. She clung to his coat sleeve by way of thanking him but he did not like that. He left abruptly and said to help ourselves to the black plums as well. On our way home the others made fun of him, made fun of his wart, and the unmatching buttons on his coat.

'And what about his anatomy,' Mabel said and we all burst out laughing though we did not know why.

He appeared the last night of the carnival, danced with the two elderly Protestant girls, excelled himself at the rifle range and won a jug which he gave to Mabel. She had been trailing around after him the whole evening and asked him up for the Ladies' Choice. No one knows for sure if they went behind the tent but they were missing for a while, and the following day Mabel was trembling with excitement. She told everyone that Matt 'had what it takes'. She had a home perm which did not suit her and also she wrote to the woollen mills to ask if they had remnants sufficient to make two-pieces, or three-pieces, and in anticipation she reserved the dressmaker. The money for these fripperies came from the few remaining bonds that she cashed. Her mother did not know. Her father did not know. I thought how courageous in a way was her recklessness. She was younger, giddier and in good spirits with everybody. One morning she met me on my way to school. There was a light frost and the plumes of grass looked like ostrich feathers. Feeling my bare hands she said that she would knit me gloves before the winter. I wondered why she was so affectionate.

Then came the command. I was to get away early from school and I was to tell the teacher that we were expecting visitors, hence I had to help my mother with sausage rolls and dainties. I dreaded telling a lie but she had a hold over me because of my impersonation of the dummies. She told me where to meet her and what time. There was a downpour after lunch and when I came upon her she was cursing the rain, cursing the fates and putting her hands up to protect her frizzled hair. Her hair hung in wet absurd ringlets over her forehead and made her look like a crabbed doll.

'What the hell kept you,' she said and started to walk. Before long I learnt that I was to take a letter to Matt. She conveyed me some of the way and then crouched against a wall to wait. There was a roaring wind and she looked pathetic as she huddled there in suspense.

'Take the short cut, through the woods,' she said. It was an old wood and dark as an underworld. In the wind the branches swayed and even the boughs seemed to waver. Every time a bird chirped or every time a branch snapped I thought it was some monster come to tackle me. I talked out loud to keep things at bay, I shouted, I ran and at moments doubted if I would ever get there. The thought of her hatched beneath a wall in her good coat, reeking of perfume, drove me on. The perfume was called Californian Poppy and it had a smell of carnations. I could barely distinguish the path through the wood so obscure was it, and briars barred the way. My heart gave a leap of joy when I saw the three chimney pots and realised that I was almost there. The house seemed even lonelier than on the first day. Everything – the hall door, the stone itself, the window frames – everything was green and sodden from rain. It looked a picture of desolation, a house with no other houses to buffet or befriend it and no woman to hang curtains or put pots of geraniums on the sill. It would have been ghostly except for the fowl and the snorting of the pigs. I reckoned they would kill the pigs for Christmas. Matt was not at home. His brother gaped through the window, then drew the bolt back and peered out and said without being asked, 'He's gone to Gort and won't be back.' I feared now of some worse incident, so I thrust the note into his hand, bolted down the yard, did not wait to close the iron gate, and hurried into the woods which by comparison were safe.

Mabel was livid. She called me every name under the sun. An eejit, a fool, a dunce, an imbecile. She wanted me to go back for the letter but I said the brother would have read it by now and going back would only show that we were culpable.

'You little poltroon,' she said and I thought she would brain me with the point of a stick which she brandished and prodded in the air. The rain had stopped but the drops came in sudden bursts from the trees and each time she ducked to protect her hair. Our walk home was wretched. Not a word passed between us. The only thing I heard was an occasional smack as she clacked her tongue against the roof of her mouth to verify her rage. We parted company as we got to the town and she said that was the last time we would be seen walking together. I did not plead with her knowing that it was in vain. Poor Mabel. It was pitiful to think of how she had dressed up and had worn uncomfortable court shoes under her galoshes and had been lavish with the perfume, all to no avail. But I could not tell her I pitied her as she would have exploded. I don't know what she did then, whether she went back to search for him or went into the chapel to give outlet to her grief. She might even have called on her friend the lady publican for a few glasses of port. All I know is that she stopped speaking to me and when we met on the road she would give a toss of her head and look in the opposite direction. Sundays reverted to being long dull days when one waited fruitlessly for a caller.

After Christmas there was a ghastly rumour and it was that Mabel was having a baby. It resounded throughout the parish. It was at first hotly denied by Mabel's mother who was told it in the strictest confidence by my mother. Mabel had grown a bit stout her mother conceded but that was because she ate too much griddle bread. The denial and the excuse pacified people but not for long. Within a month Mabel had swelled and one day a few of the women set a terrible trap for her. Polly the ex-midwife, and her nearest neighbour, who had fainted upon hearing of Mabel's downfall, enlisted Rita, a young girl, to help in their ruse.

The plan was that they would invite Mabel to tea, flatter her by telling her how thin she looked, and then having put her off guard, Rita was to steal up on her from behind and put a measuring tape around her waist. It turned out that Mabel was huge and by nightfall the conclusion was that Mabel was indeed having a baby. After that she was shunned at Mass, shunned on her way down from Mass, and avoided when she went into the shops. People were weird in the punishments they thought should be meted out to her. Throughout all this Mabel did nothing but grin and smile and say what marvellous weather it was. If people were too snooty, she went up to them and said, 'Go on, tell me what you're thinking of me.' She would dare them to give an opinion. My mother said that it would be a mercy if someone were to take a stick to Mabel and her mother said that when Mabel's father got to hear of it he would kick her arse through the town. Mabel had few friends – the lady publican, the postman who himself had once got a girl into trouble, and the dummies who mauled her as she came out of Mass not knowing that she was to be ostracised. She went to the town at all hours and cadged cigarettes off the men once they were drunk.

'Whose is it, Mabel?' she was asked by one of these drunkards.

'Your guess is as good as mine,' she said, manifesting no shame at all. She did not go to see Matt and she did not even mention him. He kept to himself and was not seen at Mass. Strange that a posse of men led by her father did not go either. It may have been because Matt was superior, having been to Canada, and also he kept a shotgun and might fire as they came through the yard. The Priest promised her mother that he would go when the weather got finer but he kept putting it off and instead made a most lurid sermon about impurity. The women in the congregation coughed, blushed and were deeply affected by it. All Mabel did was smirk and cross her legs which was a disrespectful thing to do in a holy place. It was decided that she was losing her reason, and hence her outrageous behaviour. She alternated between being very talkative and being gloomy. She sat in the hen-house for hours smoking and brooding. Getting cigarettes was at that time one of her biggest problems because she had extended her credit in all the shops. She asked me if ever I got a shilling or found money to get her a packet of fags. Then she made me listen at the wall of her stomach and said wasn't it full of mischief.

My parents were enlisted to help. A stranger was to come to our house and I was not sure what he was to do for Mabel, but he was crucial. A man in a long brown leather coat and matching gauntlet gloves arrived in his motor just before dark. He was shown into the front room where my parents and Mabel's mother spoke to him. Mabel was with me in the kitchen where she did nothing but make faces. She had discovered the satisfaction of making faces. She scrunched up her nose, stuck out her tongue and rolled her eyes in all directions.

'I can paddle my own canoe,' she said as she paced back and forth. Watching her I kept imagining the most terrible metamorphosis going on inside her and tried to calculate how old the thing was. She asked if the people up the street ever spoke about her and I lied by saying no. She said a lot of people had a lot of bees in their bonnet but yet when they reproached her, she quailed. She went in with bowed head and bowed back. Presently my mother came out and said to lay a tray quickly. She was surprisingly cheerful as if he had promised to perform a miracle. She bustled about the kitchen and said what a mercy it was that we did not have such a cross to bear. Then she asked me to put a doily on the cake plate and to make sure that the cake knife had no mould or rust.

To this day I do not know whether the stranger was a faith healer, or a quack, or perhaps a bachelor in search of a wife. At any rate after he left, spirits sagged. There was another consortium and it was decided that they would tell Mabel's father that night. His shock upon hearing it was such that he could be heard roaring half a mile away and it seems it took three people to hold him down as he threatened to go to Mabel's room in order to kill her. Gradually he was mollified with hot whiskey and the assurance that the event had happened in the most untoward and unfortunate way, in short that Mabel had been molested by a stranger. Thus, rage was transferred to a brute who had come and gone and now Mabel was told to come down and eat her supper. It seems she sat hunched over the fire snivelling and fiddling with the tongs while her father ranted. He had somehow got it into his head that it was a tinker who had done the deed and he cursed every member of that fraternity both male and female. He was made to swear that he would not strike her and when my parents left, the family were as happy as might be expected under such woeful circumstances.

The next day Mabel's mother went to the town to buy wool and in her spare time she began to knit vests, matinee coats and little boots. But it could not be said that she and Mabel became reconciled. Her mother would sit out in the yard scraping the ground with a stone or a stick, making Vs and circles and asking her Maker to take pity on her. Not a word passed between the two women, only growls. When the mother came into the kitchen Mabel went out to the hen-house. No one knew where the birth would take place and no one knew when. No arrangements were made. Mabel got highly strung when asked and burst into tears and said that no one in the whole wide world loved or understood her. She was a sight, in a brown tweed coat and a knitted cap. Being large did not become her and in contrast her face looked minute. She went to the chapel every afternoon as if to atone, and as it got nearer her time people were less vicious about her.

It was a summer's day and the men were in the hay field when Mabel's labour commenced. The Angelus had just struck. As her mother heard the first howl she ran with the tongs still in her hand on to the road for help. She hailed a passing cyclist and told him to get the doctor quick. The doctor, who was a locum, was bound to be in the dispensary at that hour. I was nearby playing shop with two of my friends and we were sent to fetch my mother. Soon pots of water were boiled, Mabel was crying and begging for ether. My friends and I were both drawn to the house and repelled by it. At every sound Mabel's mother asked was it coming, yet she avoided going into the room. She merely called in through the open door. Mabel was becoming delirious as the pains got worse, but mercifully we saw the doctor arrive. He was brusque, asked what the trouble was and said 'tch ... tch ... tch' when told.

'Why haven't I seen her sooner?' he said and then frowned as if he decided that everyone in the neighbourhood was wanting. Mabel was howling as he entered but soon after a calm descended and we remained in the kitchen full of suspense, and muttering a prayer. It was not long until he came out.

'You can put that stuff away,' he said referring to the swaddling clothes and the aluminium bath that was filled with water. Mabel's mother concluded that the infant was dead and said, 'Lord have mercy on its soul.'

'There is no *it*,' he said. 'She's no more pregnant than I am.'

My mother and Mabel's mother were aghast. It was as if some terrible trick had been played on them. Naturally they were incredulous.

'There's nothing there, I've examined her.'

'But Doctor, is that possible?' my mother asked accusingly.

'It's all hogwash,' he said. He did not know the circumstances and nobody bothered to tell him. He simply said that it was a pity he had not been consulted sooner and then announced that his fee would be two pounds and he'd like it there and then. From the room the crying had stopped and no one took the slightest trouble to go in. No one went near her. It was as if she had taken on the marks of a leper. Her mother glared in that direction and said that her only daughter had brought them nothing but disaster. To have to tell this to the parish was the last straw. The waves in her white hair bristled and she reminded me of nothing so much as a weasel, poised to spit. Her withheld temper was worse than all her husband's exclaiming.

'Let her break it to him herself,' she said pointing a fist towards the closed door. If one can curse in silence she did it then, so resolute and so full of hatred was her expression. By way of consolation my mother said that surely Mabel could not be right in the head. Her words were hardly a solace.

From the room now there was a low keen. No doubt Mabel was still lying down, and bunched up as she had been in labour and perhaps waiting for a kind word. No one ventured in. Her mother emptied the tea leaves into the front garden and with a swish told my two friends, who had been waiting outside, to vamoose. Back in the kitchen she began to list Mabel's faults and lament the money she had cost them since she came home. Money on tonics, money on style, money on faddish food when she got those cravings at night.

'Tinned salmon no less,' she said sourly and told my mother that her pension each week had gone towards Mabel's whim. Then for no reason she recalled a large beautiful hand-painted urn that Mabel had broken when young. It seems that from the confines of her pram Mabel had reached up to embrace it and toppled it instead. This announcement seemed to confirm that Mabel was, from birth, a rotten egg. Mabel's attraction to the opposite sex had been in the nature of a disease.

It would be funny to see her thin, having just seen her that morning large and cumbersome. The rush crib was still on the kitchen table and the sight of it an affront. I wanted to bring her a slice of cake, or tea in her favourite china cup, but I was afraid to disobey them. I felt that this now would be as much a quality of mine as my eyes or my hair, this paralysis in my character, this wanting to step in but not daring to. I would, I wouldn't. Thus I wrestled but the weight and depth of their approbrium won and I did not go in, nor did they, and the whimpering went on, the chant of a hopeless creature.

We did not lay eyes on Mabel again. Just as the shame of pregnancy had made her brazen and untoward, so now the shame of non-pregnancy had made her withdraw. She refused to see anyone and barely broke her fast. One evening, after dark, she left as she had once arrived, in a hackney car and from that moment her memory was banished. The only reminder was that next day on the clothes line were her blankets, her patchwork quilt and some baby clothes. Her parents had a Mass said in the house and in time it was as if she had never come home, as if she were still in Australia.

Some said that she was in Dublin working for nuns, others said that she worked in a nursing home, and still others that she was a charwoman. These were just stories. No one ever knew the real truth and it is possible that Mabel herself did not know it, but died, as she had lived, a simpleton.

Courtship

A favourite school poem was 'The Mother' by Patrick Pearce. It was a wrenching poem condoling the plight of a mother who had seen her two strong sons go out and die, 'in bloody protest for a glorious thing'. Mrs Flynn had also known tragedy, her husband having died from pleurisy and her younger son Frank had drowned while away on holiday. For a time she wept and gnashed; her fate being similar to the poor distraught 'Mother' in the poem. I did not know her then but there were stories of how she baulked at hearing the tragic news. When the Guards came to tell her that Frank was drowned she simply pressed her hands to her ears and ran out of the house, into the garden, saying to leave her alone, to stop pestering people. When at last they made her listen, her screaming was such that the Curate heard it two miles away. Her son was eighteen and very brainy.

By the time I met her she seemed calm and reconciled, a busy woman, who owned a shop and a mill and who had three other sons, all of whom were over six feet and who seemed gigantic beside her, because she was a diminutive woman with grey permed hair. Her pride in them was obvious and transmitted itself to all who knew her. It was not anything she said, it was just the way she would look up at them as if they were a breed of gods, and sometimes she would take a clothes brush and brush one of their lapels, just to confirm that closeness. They all had dark eyes and thick curly hair and there was not a girl in the parish who did not dream of being courted by one of them. Of the three, Michael was the most sought after. It was his lovely manner, as the women said, even the old women melted when they described how he put them at their ease when they went to sell eggs or buy groceries. He was a famous hurley player and the wizard way that he scored a goal was renowned and immortalised in verses, that the men carried in their pockets. If his team were ever in danger of losing, and he had been put off for a foul – as he often was – the crowd would clamour for him and the referee had no choice but to let him back. His speciality was to score a goal in the very last minute of the game when the opposing team had thought themselves certain of victory; and this goal and the eerie way in which it was scored would be a talking point for weeks. Then after the match the fans would carry him on their shoulders, and the crowd would mill round, trying to touch his feet or his hands, just as in the Gospels the crowd milled about trying to touch Our Lord. That night in a dance hall, girls would vie to dance with him. He had a steady girl called Moira but when he travelled to hurling matches he met other girls at dances and for weeks, some new girl, some Ellen, or some Dolly, or some Kate, would plague him with love letters. I learnt this from Peggy, their maid, when I went there on my first ever holiday. I had yearned to go for many years and at last the chance came, because my sister, who used to go, had set her sights on the city and went instead to cousins in Limerick who had a sweet shop that adjoined a chip shop. As in many other things I had taken her place; I was her substitute and the realisation of this was not without its undercurrent of jealousy and pique.

On my first day in their house I felt very gawky, and kept avoiding the brothers and crying in the passage. I wanted to go home but was too ashamed to mention it. It was Michael who rescued me.

'Will you do me a favour?' he said.

The favour was very simple – it was to make him apple fritters. If there was anything in the world he craved it was apple fritters. I was to make them surreptitiously, when his mother was not looking.

'Can't,' I said.

His mother and Peggy were constantly about and the thought of defying them quite impossible.

'Suppose they went off for a day, would you make them then?'

'Of course.'

That 'Of course', so quick, so yielding, and already making it clear that I was eager to serve him.

In a matter of days I had settled in and thought no place on earth so thrilling and so bustling as their house and their shop. They stocked everything – groceries, animal feed, serge for suits, winceyette, cotton, paraffin, cakes, confectionery, boots, wellingtons, and cable-knit sweaters that were made by spinsters and lonely women up the mountains. They even sold underwear for ladies and gents and these were the subject of much innuendo and mirth. The ladies' corsets were of pink broderie anglaise and sometimes one of the brothers would take one out of its cellophane and put it on, over his trousers, as a joke. Of course that was when the shop was empty and his mother had gone to Confession, or to see a sick neighbour. They respected their mother and in her presence never resorted to shady language.

What I liked about staying there was the jokes, the levity, and the constant activity – cakes being delivered, meal being weighed, eggs being brought in and having to be counted as well as washed, orders having to be got ready and at any moment a compliment or a pinch in the arm from one of the brothers. It was all so exhilarating. At night more diversion, when the men convened in the back bar, drank porter and talked in monosyllables until they got drunk and then ranted and raved, and got obstreperous when it came to politics. If they were too unruly Michael would roll up his sleeves, take off his wristwatch and tell them that unless they 'cut out the bull' they would be rudely ejected to the yard outside.

In the morning the brothers joked and made references to the dramas of the night before, while their mother always said it was inviting disaster to have men in, after hours. The Guards rarely raided because of once having to give the terrible news about Frank but she was always in fear that she might be raided, disgraced and brought to court. The brothers used to tease her about being a favourite with the Sergeant and though pretending to resent this she blushed and got very agitated and looked in all directions so as to avoid their insinuations. I wore a clean dress each day and to enhance myself a starched white collar which gave me, I thought, a plaintive look. I was forever plying them with more tea or another fried egg or relish. Michael would touch my wrist and say, 'That the girl, that the girl', and I hoped that I would never have to go home. I even harboured a dream about being adopted by his mother so that I would become his sister and shake hands with him, or even embrace, without any suggestion of shame or sin.

Each morning the elder brother, William, filled the buggy with provisions in order to go up the country to buy and to sell. He used to coax me to go with him by telling me about the strange people he met. In one house three members of the family were mad and bayed like dogs and the fourth, sane, member had to throw buckets of water on them to calm them down. There was the house or rather the hovel where the hunchback, Della, lived, and she constantly invited him in for tea in the hope that he would propose to her. Each time when he refused Della stamped her foot and said that the invitation wasn't meant anyhow. There was a mother and daughter who never stirred out of bed and who called to him to come upstairs where he would find them in bed, wearing fancy bed-jackets, with rouge and lipstick on them, consulting fashion catalogues.

'Do you ever score?' I heard his cousin Tom ask him one morning, and William put his fingers to his lips and smiled as if there were sagas he could tell. But I would not be dragged to these places because for one thing I had no interest in fields or hay-sheds or lakes, and for another I wanted to remain in Michael's orbit and be ready at any moment should he summon me, or just bump into me and give me a sudden thrilling squeeze. He worked in the mill which was a short distance across the garden. Sometimes I would convey him out there and if the birds were gorging on the currant bushes, as they usually were, he would flap his hands and make a great to-do as he frightened them away.

'Be seeing you later, alligator,' he always said and lifted his cap once or twice to show that he was a gentleman. I then had to go back and help Peggy to wash the dishes, polish the range and scrub the kitchen and the back kitchen. Later we made the beds. Making his bed was exciting but untoward. Peggy would flare up as she entered the room, then she would whip the bedclothes off and grumpily shake them out of the window. In the yard below the geese cackled when she shook these bed-clothes and the gander hissed and raised his orange beak to defend his tribe.

'I can't wait to get to England,' Peggy would say, and her version of life there seemed to envisage a world that did not include geese or the necessity to make beds. The room itself was like all the bedrooms, high-ceilinged, covered with garish carpet and unmatching furniture. There was the dark mahogany wardrobe with a long mirror that looked muddied over and gave back a very poor and faulty reflection of the self. There was the double bed with wooden headboard and there was a cane chair beside the bed on which he flung clothes. His shoes, so big and so important, were laid inside the kerb of the tiled fireplace, tan shoes well shone and with shoe-trees in them, his fawn coat on a hanger, swaying a little in the dark space of the wardrobe. There were too his various ties, the red-tasselled box in which were thrown the several love letters, his scapulars, his missal and then most nakedly of all, his pyjamas in a heap at the end of the very tossed bed, causing Peggy to be incensed and to ask aloud if he played hurley in his sleep or what. Along the mantelpiece was the row of cups that he had won at hurley and beside them a framed photograph of his mother as a very young girl with lips pouted, like a rosebud. I would touch the cups and beg of Peggy to tell me when and where each one had been awarded. They were tarnished and I resolved that one day I would get silver dip and put such a shine on them that when he entered his room that night he would be greeted by the gleam of silver and would wonder who had done it and maybe would even find out.

Once the beds were done I would then concoct an excuse to go over to the mill. Up to the moment I had yielded I would intend not to go, but then all of a sudden some frenzied need would take hold of me and though despising myself for such weakness, I succumbed. Crossing the garden, humming some stupid ditty I would already picture him, his face and jacket dusted over with white grain, his whole being smelling of it, his skin powdered and pale, a feature which made him look older but made his eyes shine like deep pools. I would hear the rush of the little river and see segments of it being splashed and tumbled in the spokes of the big wooden mossy mill wheel and I would go in trying to appear casual.

'Any news,' he would say and invariably he asked if the English folk had been yet to the shop. An Englishman and his son had come to the district to shoot, and fish; and their accents were a source of mirth to us, as was their amazement about nature. They were most surprised by the fact that they had caught a rabbit, and brought it over to show it to people as if it were a trophy.

One day however I found him in a rage, and saw that he was hitting the wooden desk and calling Jock, the boy who helped him, the greatest idiot under the sun. Michael had addressed the bills to his customers and had put 'Esquire' after each one when Jock had come along and put 'Mr' before each name and now thirty or forty envelopes would have to be re-addressed. Despite his fury he had put his arm around me as usual and said what a pity that I couldn't work in the mill, so's he'd send Jock to a reformatory where he belonged. I was basking in being so close to him when a beautiful older girl sauntered in, on the very flimsy excuse that she was looking for her father. This was Eileen, with blonde hair, blue eyes and great long black lashes which she knowingly flaunted by repeated fluttering. She worked in Dublin but was home for a few days and as she came down between the sacks it was prodigal to see their interest in each other quicken. She walked with a sway and said that her father was supposed to have come with bags of corn for grinding but where on earth had he vanished to? Seeing his arm around me she pretended to be very haughty and said 'Sorry', then turned on her heel and walked away. She wore a red jacket, a pleated skirt and wedge-heeled canvas sandals with straps that laced up over her calves.

'What's the big hurry,' he called out to her.

'Have to see a man about a dog,' she said and she turned and smirked. He said that he had not known she was at home and might he ask how long would the parish have the pleasure of her exotic company.

'Until I get the wanderlust,' she said and announced that she might go to a hotel at the seaside for a weekend as she heard they had singsongs.

'God, you must be rolling in it,' he said.

'Correct,' she said and put out her arm to reveal the bone bangles that she wore.

'I suppose we're the country mohawks,' he said.

'You certainly don't know how to pamper a girl,' she said and implied that men in Dublin knew what it was all about. The peals of laughter that she let out were at once sweet and audacious.

'Do you live on the north side?' he said.

'Gosh, no, the south side,' she said and added that if one lived on the north side one would be roused by the bawling of cattle two mornings a week as they were driven to the cattle market, and herded into pens. 'The north side is far too countrified,' she said.

'So you're sitting pretty on the south side,' he said with a sting. By now he had deserted me and was facing her, taking such stock of her as if every detail of her person intrigued him. Though they were saying caustic things, they were playful and revelled in each other's banter.

'Who's the little kid?' she said, looking back at me and

upon being told she said that she knew my sister, had seen her at dances and that my sister was full of herself.

'What are you up to, tonight?' he asked.

'Fast work,' she said and he biffed her and then they linked and went outside, to confer. Standing next to Jock who was scratching the 'Mr' off each envelope I felt foolish, felt outcast just like him. They stood in the doorway close together and fired with curiosity I hurried towards them and slipped out without even being noticed. There was a lorry parked to one side and I stood on the running board in order to spy on them. It was awful. His arm was around her waist and she was looking up at him, saying, 'What do *you* think you're doing.' He said he could do as he pleased, break her ribs if he felt like it.

'Just try, just you try,' she said and with both hands he appeared to mash her ribs as he circled her waist. A few flies droned around the lorry as there were milk tanks on the back and there was a smell of sour milk and metal. The driver's seat was torn and bits of spiral spring stuck out of it. I wondered whose lorry it was. Not having looked for a few minutes I now allowed myself another glance at the bewitched pair. He was now standing a little behind her, her pleated skirt was raised so that it came unevenly above her knees and I could see the top of her legs, the lace of her slip and her mounting excitement as she stood on tip-toe to accommodate herself to what he was doing. Also she let out suggestive sounds and was laughing and wriggling until suddenly she became very matter of fact, pulled her skirt down and said what did he think he was up to. Then she ran off but he caught her and they had a little tug of war. He let go of her on the understanding that they would meet that night and they made an appointment in the grounds of what had once been a demesne, but was now gone to ruin.

By the time they met and possibly just as he was resting their two bicycles, interlocking them, against a tree, or spreading his overcoat on the grass, I was kneeling down to say the Rosary with his mother whose voice throbbed with devotion. She had decided that night to offer up the Rosary for her dead son and her dead husband. The kitchen flagstones felt hard and grimy and it was as if grit was being ground into our knees as we recited endless Our Fathers, Hail Marys and Glory Be's. I was thinking of the lovers with a curiosity that bordered on frenzy. I could picture the meeting place, the smell of grass, cows wheezing, their two faces, almost featureless in the dark, and by not being able to see, their power of touch so overwhelmingly whetted, that their hands reached out, and suddenly they clove together and dared to say each other's Christian name with a hectic urgency. I was thinking this while at the same time mouthing the prayers and hearing the mumbling of the men in the bar outside. I even knew the men who were there and saw one old man to whom I had an aversion, because the porter froth made gold foam on his grey moustache. Mrs Flynn was profligate that night with prayers and insisted that we do the Three Mysteries, the Joyful, Sorrowful and Glorious. It was after ten o'clock when we stood up and we were both doubled over from the hours of kneeling.

She asked if as a reward I would like a 'saussie', and she popped two sausages into the pan that was always lying on the side of the stove in case any of her sons became hungry. In no time the fat was hissing and she was prodding the sausages with a fork and telling them to hurry up as there were two famished customers. Afterwards she gave me little biscuits with coloured icing and said that I could come for every holiday and stay for the entire length. Saying it, I think she believed that I would never grow up. I slept with her and all that I recall of the bedroom is that it was damp, that the flowered wallpaper had become runny and disfigured, and that the feathers in the pillows used to dig into one's flesh. That night, perhaps exalted from so much praying she did not insist that we go to sleep at once but allowed us to chat. Naturally I brought the subject around to her sons.

'Which of them do you prefer?' I asked.

'They're all the same in my eyes,' she said in a very practical voice.

'But isn't Michael a great hurler,' I said, hoping that

we could discuss him, hoping she would tell me what he was like as a baby, and as a little boy, what mischief he had done, and maybe even discuss his present behaviour, especially his gallivanting.

She said that a gypsy came into the shop one day long ago and predicted that Michael would have a checkered life and that she prayed hourly that he would never take it into his head to go to England.

'He won't,' I said without any justification.

'Please God not,' she said and added that Michael was a softie with everybody. Little did she know that at that moment he was engaged in a clinch that would make her writhe.

'I think he is your favourite,' I said.

'What a little imp you are,' she said and announced that we must go to sleep at once. But I knew that I wouldn't. I knew that I would stay awake until I heard him come up the stairs and go into his room, and that having heard him I would experience some remote satisfaction, thinking, or rather hoping that he had tired of Eileen, and was now ours again. It was very late when he got back and my mood was dismal because of his whistling. A mad notion took hold of me to go and ask him if he wanted sausages, but mercifully I resisted.

I wondered which of the two girls he would smile at, next day at Mass. As it happened Eileen and his girl friend Moira were in the same seat, but not next to one another. Eileen was all in black, with a black mantilla that shrouded her face. I thought she looked ashamed but I may have imagined it. Moira had a cardigan knitted in the blackberry stitch and a matching beret that was clapped on the side of her head and secured with a pearled hat pin. During the long sermon she kept turning round, probably to see where Michael was. He stood in the back of the church with the men, and like them skidaddled at the last Gospel. The two girls came down the aisle very quietly and exchanged a word in the porch. Then Moira went on home with her parents, and Eileen cycled home alone.

.   .   .   .   .

At lunchtime Michael was very attentive to me, kept giving me more gravy and more roast potatoes, kept telling me to eat up. It was my last day as I was leaving very early in the morning on the mail car. Perhaps he was nice to me for that reason or else it was a silent bribe not to betray his secret. I had already accrued a gift of ten shillings, and a rosary beads from his mother; in the back of the crucifix was a little cavity containing a special relic.

As we were eating, their cousin Tom rushed into the kitchen and announced that he was taking me to the pictures that night. The brothers let out some hoots, whereupon he said that for two weeks I had helped in the kitchen, helped in the shop, and had had no diversion at all. To my dismay their mother applauded the idea and said what a shame that one of her sons hadn't shown such thought. I disliked Tom, he had a smile that was faintly indecent and whenever a girl went by, he made licking sounds and gurgles. He had glaring red hair, pale skin with freckles and often he wore his socks up over his trouser legs to emphasise his calves. His hands were the most revolting, being very white, and his fingers were like long white slugs. Despite the fact that I withered at being invited he said that he would pick me up at six and that we would have a whale of a time. The cinema was three or four miles away and we were to cycle. I dreaded cycling, as even in the daylight I had a tendency to wobble. The Angelus was striking as he arrived in a green tweed suit with matching cap. He was unable to conceal his pleasure and at once I saw his salaciousness from the way he touched the saddle of my bicycle and said oughtn't I to have a little cover on it, as it wasn't soft enough. 'You demon,' Michael said to him as we set off. The cycling was most unnerving and I bumped into him several times and found myself veering to the ditch whenever a car passed us. He said that had he known of my precariousness he would have put a cushion on the crossbar and conveyed me himself. I could not bear his voice and I could not bear his unctuousness, and what I disliked most of all was the way he kept saying my name, making it clear that he was attracted to me.

When we got to the cinema he linked me up the steps and led me into the foyer. It was a very luxurious place with a wide stairs and the streams of light from the big chandelier made rainbow prisms on the red carpet. The stair handle had just been polished and it smelt of Brasso. Inside he settled us into two seats in the second last row and once it became dark he grasped my hand and began to squeeze it. I pretended not to know what was going on. His next ruse was to tickle the palm of my hand slowly with his fingers. A woman had told me that if tickled on the palm of the hand, or behind the knees, one could become wanton and lose control. On the screen Lola Montez was engaged in the most strenuous and alarming scuffles as she tried to escape a villain. Her predicament was not unlike my own. Having attacked the palm of one hand he then set out on the other and finding me unwilling, if not to say recalcitrant, he told me to uncross my legs, but I wouldn't. I sealed them together and wound one foot around the other ankle so that I was like something stitched together. I strove to ignore him, and annoyed by this he leaned over and licked my ear and so revolted me that I let out a cry causing people to turn around in amazement. Naturally he drew away and when the man behind him thumped his shoulder he muttered some abject apology about his sister (that was me) being very highly strung.

When we left the cinema he was livid. He said why do such a thing, why egg him on with ringlets and smiles and then make a holy show of him. I said sorry. What with the dark, and the long cycle home I realised that I was at his mercy. I feigned great interest in the plot of the film and began to question him about it but he saw through this ruse and suddenly swerved his bicycle in front of mine and said 'Halt, halt.' I knew what it presaged. He took both bicycles, slung them aside and then embraced me and said what a little 'tease' I was, and then backed me towards a gateway. The gate rattled and shook under the impact of our joined bodies and from inside the field a cow let out a very lugubrious moan.

'I'm not going in there,' I said.

'Not half,' he said.

He said he had paid three and sixpence per seat and had had enough codology and wasn't taking any more. I summoned all the temerity I could, and said how the priest would kill me and also Mrs Flynn would kill me.

'They needn't know,' he said.

'They would, they would,' I said.

He was not going to be fobbed off with excuses.

'Have a heart!' he said as he began to kiss me, and enquire what colour underclothes I wore.

'I love Michael, I love Michael,' I said vehemently. Foolishly I thought jealousy might quell his intentions.

'Hasn't he got Moira,' he said and went on to outline how Michael was at that very moment in the loft above the mill, close to Moira, a rendezvous they kept most Sunday nights.

'That's a lie,' I said.

'Is it!' he said and boasted how Michael described Moira's arrival, her shyness, her chatter, then her capitulation as he removed her coat, her dress, her underclothes and she lay there with not a stitch. As his advances were now rapid, I knew there was nothing for it but to have a fit. I started to shake all over, to scream, to say disjointed things, indeed to be so delirious that he slapped me on the face and said for Christ's sake to calm down, that no one was going to do anything to me. We could hear a car in the distance and as its headlights came around the corner I ran out and waved frantically. It was the Vet who slowed down, wound the window and shouted 'What's up?'

'Nothing's up,' Tom said and added that I had a puncture but that he had mended it. When the car drove off he picked up his bicycle and said for a long time he had not had such a fiasco of an evening.

Ours was a silent and a sullen journey home. He cycled ahead of me and never once turned round to see if I followed. As we neared the village he cycled on downhill and I got off because my brakes were faulty. I felt full of shame and blunder and did not know what I would say if Mrs Flynn or the brothers asked me if I had enjoyed myself. I felt disgraced and dearly wished that I could go home there and then.

Michael confronted me in the hall as I was hanging up my coat. He said had I seen a ghost or what, as I was white as a sheet. Soon he guessed.

'The pup, the blackguard,' he said as he brought me into the kitchen. He put me on the big armchair, sat beside me, and started to stroke my hair, all the while iterating what injury he would do to Tom. Suddenly he kissed me, and this kiss being a comfort he followed it with a shower of kisses, embraces and fond fugitive words.

'I love you,' I said bluntly.

'Ditto,' he said. His voice and expression were quite different now, young and unguarded. I was seeing the man for whom Moira, Eileen and a host of girls would tear each other's eyes out. We heard a stir and he drew back, stood up sharply, and opened the kitchen door very casually, while also winking at me.

'Who goes there?' he said in a stern voice and then went into the well of the hall but no one answered. He crossed over into the shop and all of a sudden the kitchen became dark, either because he had interfered with the mains, or their electricity plant had gone wrong. I was like someone in a trance. I could feel him coming back by his soft quick steps and then by the glow of a cigarette. Just as I had once imagined the lure of his voice in the dark saying a name, he now said mine and his arms reached out to me with a sweet, almost a childlike supplicatingness. What had been disgusting and repellent an hour before was now a transport and there was nothing for it but to be glad; that wild and frightened gladness that comes from breaking out of one's lonely crust, and just as with the swimmer who first braves the depths, the fear is secondary to the sense of prodigal adventure. He said that he would get some cider and two glasses and that we could go over to the loft where no one would bother us. Whatever he proposed I would have agreed.

We went out like thieves and crossing the yard he picked me up so's I wouldn't spoil my shoes.

In the morning he stuck his tousled head out of his bed-room door, and in front of his mother gave me a quick kiss, then whispered, 'I'll be waiting for you.' It was not true but it was all I wanted to hear and on the drive home, the blue misted hills, the cold lakes, the songs of the birds, and the shiny laurel hedges around the grand estates, all seemed startlingly beauti-ful and energised and it was as if they had just been inhabited by some new and thrilling life.

Ghosts

Three women. They represent defiance, glamour and a kind of innocence that I miss in my later world. They were all tall and if I had to liken them to anything it would be to those paintings of winter trees, with scarcely a leaf left, trees shorn by the wind.

The first of them went periodically mad, and one day during one of those bouts she walked into our kitchen wielding an ash plant. Our back door was always open, and there was an odd wellington boot to it to keep it ajar. She was called Delia, and at once she struck out at everything she could see. Her consummate anger was vented on our pale elm dresser, and I worried for the beautiful plates that were wedged in along the back. They were plates that my mother had won at a carnival in Coney Island long before. They were the nicest thing in the whole kitchen. They were white china plates with a different flower on each one. The plate I loved most had a strange spiral flower that was not like the flowers that grew in the fields. I feared for all of them but principally for it. Delia lashed out and said that they were dirty, filthy, said that the whole place was a dive and full of muck and that she was going to see to it that we cleaned our premises. I went in under the table, a place I often resorted to, and where pups or dogs often followed.

On she went, expressing her dislike of our way of life, of my mother's brown bread – she made horrible faces, as if she were taking cascara – of the oilcloth on the table, of the dust in the brown corduroy cushions on the armchair. As far as we knew, her own house was a pigsty. She lived there with her two brothers and an invalid mother, and no one ever cleaned it. The Veterinary Surgeon used to say that he had to fumigate himself after he had been to their back kitchen to get hot water or his fee. Their house was called Bracken House, and there was a river nearby. It flooded in the winter, and their fields were swampy. They had an old piano in the sitting-room, and there they kept bags of sugar and flour and also a machine in which they pulped mangels and turnips. Their voices were forever raised. That was all we knew about them, and when we children had occasion to pass their gateway we would run, and tell each other that the maddies had come to catch us. Her brother Dinny used to chase girls and ask them into the hay-shed to romp. He, too, used to be carted to the asylum.

Now Delia was in our house and behaving as if she were a governess, as if she had a right to open cupboards and object to spilled sugar or spilled oatmeal and to say 'disgusting', and repeat it until she was singing it on a very high wavery note. It was just as well we did not own a piano or have our concertina. The local sergeant had borrowed it for a wedding.

My mother calmed her by sitting her down and giving her a mug of tea and cake. It was a marble cake, and Delia marvelled at the three colours that composed each slice. They were like a painting, with more brown than green and the plain egg colour in the centre acting as a barrier between the two other tempting colours. My mother then showed her the green essence that she had used, and suddenly Delia became soft-spoken and our house became the loveliest nest in the world. She brooded for a moment as she chewed. She chewed very determinedly, as if she were tasting each crumb. She was a thin creature, and she wore high-heeled, laced shoes.

All of a sudden, she ventured to say that her mother and father should never have married because they were misfits. She said that her mother had only married him because he had given her 'coaxyorum'. My mother asked what that was, and Delia lowered her head and pointed to the little bottle of essence and asked if she could have a drop. After taking a spoonful of green syrup, she was all soppy and babyish, rubbing her chest in slow circular strokes. 'Coaxyorum,' she said, was like that. Long ago, her father had got up on a ladder, had gone into her mother's bedroom, had given her mother this potion, and before she knew where she was the mother was being carried down the ladder and into a sidecar and off to the father's house – in fact, to Bracken House. Her mother's family had disowned her and never spoke to her again.

Delia became so happy that at dusk she refused to go home. My mother bribed her by putting a hunk of cake in clean greaseproof paper and by giving her a pom-pom that she had taken a fancy to, but she would not budge. I remember how she clung to the brown polished bars of the chair when our workman tried to shift her, and eventually he had to threaten her with the poker, for by now we were dire enemies again and our house was a pigsty. She flounced off, threw the cake on the cement flags outside, trampled on it, and got into the cart the workman had brought round, shouting with the utmost vehemence, 'We don't need you, we don't need you, we don't bloody need you!' The last I saw of her, she was standing in the cart and then, as he got the mare into a gallop, falling down, but all the while continuing her shout of defiance. 'We don't need you, we don't bloody need you!'

The next of these women, Nancy, was a dream figure in a long motor coat and dangling from her arm a lizard handbag with a beautiful amber clasp. I can even now hear it being opened and shut as she would take out her cigarette case or her lace-edged hankie, or look in it for no reason – though perhaps it was to gaze in the little mirror in the side pocket. Every time she came to our house, she brought her own box camera, so her visits and her lovely clothes were all perpetuated, though many of them came out blurred. She was a flirt. I did not know all that it meant, but I knew that she was a flirt. She would look at men, she would drink them in, and then make a movement, or a flurry of movements, with her swallow, and she would gulp as if it were sherbet or lemonade or something fizzy. She came to our house whenever there was a dress dance in the village and she would arrive a day or two before and stay a day or two after.

The day before, she would put oatmeal packs on her face

and then a beaten egg white, and my mother and she would laugh and pose as they tried on her clothes. She always brought an attaché case full of style. There would be at least two dance dresses, her fur stole with the dark stripes that seemed in danger of coming alive or purring, two or three purses, dance shoes, and a beautiful perfume spray. I would be let hold it in my hand, let squeeze its soft, thick rubber nozzle, and presently the air of the room would be imbued with this near-religious smell and I, at least, was transported elsewhere. Sometimes she brought clothes that were on approval, and these, being new, were the most coveted and the most beautiful. She brought an astrakhan coat that she and my mother took turns trying on, and they must have tried it on ten or fifteen times one wet morning. Then I was allowed to try it on, but at once had to take it off, because it was trailing along the floor and, what with their diversion, the floor had not been swept that day and the tiles were smudged from the dogs and the men. It suited Nancy best. Her hair was auburn and copious, and this brown curly astrakhan was a perfect complement to it. She always brought her curling tongs, and when, before a dance, she started to curl her hair she would sometimes threaten to put my nose between the two warm pincers. Then her eyes would narrow and she would laugh. She was inscrutable.

She and my mother often discussed possible marriages, though she could see from my mother's life, and infer from their conversation, that marriage was not an ideal state. Still, each new man that came to the neighbourhood was a source of supreme interest to her. Not many new men came, but from time to time there was a change of staff at the bank or at the creamery, or, more rarely, a new curate. In these men she manifested great interest before she had met them at all or had any inkling what they looked like. The local county councillor was too staid for her, but my father would insist that he was a good catch, had good land and a stock of cattle. Nancy dreamed of being a receptionist in a grand hotel, of making friends with people from different walks of life and being snatched up by a foreign count or baron.

She was lazy and stayed in bed till noon. I would bring her tea and toast, and she would get me to pass her the red woolly dressing-gown, and then she would lie back with her head lolled against the brass rungs and say what a lazybones she was. I lived in dread that I might see her breasts, but mercifully her nightdress was not sheer. Her toast would be cut in neat fingers by my mother, and they seemed more mouth-watering than anything we might have downstairs. Usually we had to have brown bread, because my mother made it and it was our duty to have plain things. Toast was from shop bread and was a definite luxury. I would eat the crusts that she had left.

The new Curate, who had come fresh from the seminary, was the admiration of all. Girls blushed at the mention of his name. Nancy and he became inseparable. They would go to the shops in his baby Ford to get mutton or a sheep's head or their favourite cigarettes, and when they came back they did not get out of the car immediately but sat laughing and smoking. They chain-smoked. I never saw them touch, but as they walked towards the house it often was as if they were on the point of touching and therefore all the more tantalising. Her hand would come out of her coat pocket, or his hand might gesture towards the gate, or lift the rose briar as she stooped and stepped under it, and it needed but one more fraction for them to be in a clasp. Once, carrying either handle of a wide straw basket, they dropped it so that the grapefruit, the sugar cubes, and the tins of peas were rolling all over the flags. The grapefruit was for him, because my mother said that after the long fast for holy Mass he needed something delicate before he tackled a proper breakfast.

When Nancy was with us, he came to our house directly after Mass and stayed the whole day, until it was time to leave for the evening devotions. They would sit in the kitchen and they would talk and laugh, and Nancy would show him her style. One Sunday, she went so far as to cut his hair. It was quite a ceremony – draping him with the white towel, putting newspaper underneath, and then putting the big rusted brown scissors to his temple and going snip-snip. He was begging her to let him look in the mirror, so that he could see if she was clipping too much, but she laughed and said to trust her. As a joke, she put one of the locks of hair into a little lavallièu that she wore around her neck. The rest was swept up onto a piece of cardboard and tossed over the hedge, as tea-leaves might be. He did not like the haircut, said the congregation would now see his big ears, and so she called him Big Ears, and smiled at him, and swallowed intensely. As she commiserated with him, her eyes filled up with the most glistening tears, which she did not shed. They were like glycerine.

Sometimes she and he would call me into the kitchen and ask me to recite or tell some story about the school-teacher – how she thumped us and called us ugly names – and then just as unaccountably they would ask me to leave the kitchen at once and go outside and not come back till I was called. Those exiles into the garden were agony. They made me think of Christ in Gethsemane, and I would kneel down and ask my Maker to let such agony pass, knowing that it would not. The garden was big and windy: there was just the privet hedge, some devil's pokers, a few shrubs, and two granite pedestals that served as decoration. They were like giant mushrooms, and one of them had come unstuck from its base. I would shake it, hoping it would fall, yet dreading the fact that it might fall and yearning for a tap on the window or a 'yoo-hoo' – the signal that said come back.

The Curate escorted her to the Halloween dance and there their friendship underwent a breach. It seems he stood inside the dance-hall door, holding her fur stole, not daring to commit it to the ladies' room, lest it be stolen or tried on by the woman who minded the coats and who was dopey and lackadaisical. The dance floor was like an ice rink, and the band from County Offaly was reputed to be the best that ever came. Nancy danced with all and sundry, and each time she came to the door she smiled or gave some recognition to the Curate, who was taking stock of all the dancers but particularly of her.

For the ladies' choice she asked the county councillor, knowing that it could not give offence to her new admirer. Her new admirer was the crooner, who wore a fawn gaberdine suit

and had a lot of oil in his hair. It seems that the moment he
caught sight of her in her raspberry-coloured dress he stopped
singing, in mid-song, let out a whistle, and then pointed the
microphone in her direction. After that, he made a point of
singling her out when she approached the bandstand, and he
sang the song 'Jealousy' with a special lady in mind. When the
supper break came, she did not go down to the end of the hall
and join the Curate for lemonade and queen cakes; rather, she
sneaked out by an upper door, which was a fire exit, and was
followed by the crooner, who providently brought his Crombie
overcoat. No one knew for certain what ensued out there, save
that they were not on the grounds of the dance hall but had gone
along the road and lurked in a gateway. Nancy herself assured
my mother that it was the most harmless little thing – that they
sat on the wet wall while the crooner taught her the words of a
song she loved. She sang a bit of the chorus of it:

> *After the ball was over*
> *Just at the break of day*
> *Many's the heart that was aching*
> *If I could read them all*
> *Many's the heart that was broken*
> *Af . . . ter the ball.*

It could have been the theme song for the injured Curate,
because he did not wait to see her home. She got a lift on the
crossbar of a bicycle and got oil all over her long dress. He did
not come the next morning. My mother said that probably he
would never come, and became snappy, as she, too, loved his
visits because they lessened the undercurrent of despair that
permeated our house.

Nancy said, 'Care to bet?' And they bet sixpence. Nancy's
prediction was that he would come on the third day, and so sure
was she of this that she postponed going home until then, even
though she was needed in the city in her parents' shop. Her
parents owned a confectionery shop in Limerick and sold the
most beautiful cakes and buns. When she came to us, she
always brought a lemon cake or a chocolate cake, and once there

was an almond-flavoured cake with almond icing and a little almond chicken. She realised there was some pique on my mother's part and took to tidying two cupboards and lined them with newspaper. She picked out all the old socks too, and they looked ridiculous on the kitchen table, grey or flecked socks, all looking for a partner and most of them full of holes.

On the third morning, as the dogs ran joyously from the back steps and chased down the fields, she knew – we all knew – that it was he. She ran to the front window to make sure it was his car. My mother volunteered to go to the yard to feed the fowl, and told Nancy to lay a tray and make him feel at home.

'Hello, stranger' was what Nancy said, and she put her hand out, but he did not shake it. Her nail varnish was a rose pink and the cuticles were very defined. He sat near the range, scowling like a boy. She was all the time smiling, waiting for his rebuke so that she could dismiss it. Her hair was tied up in a big soft roll that stretched from ear to ear, and it made her look older and more sedate. It was like a big sausage. She told me to make myself scarce.

Out in the garden, I wondered what they were saying, or if they had moved nearer, or if as she marched about the kitchen to prepare his repast he was shocked by the slits in her skirt. There was a front and a back slit, and as she moved she took uncommonly large strides, so that one saw above the backs of her knees – saw the flesh covered in beige silk stockings, saw the seam going right up. I was holding the stone mushroom and was about to tilt it to one side, but the next moment I let go of it and it was bending like the Tower of Pisa. In the front room, with its long French window opening onto the garden, the most terrible thing had transpired. They had gone in there and he was stripped to the waist. He had his back to the window. She was looking at his body, as if examining it for spots or a mole or something. But what? I had to come closer in order to find out. His head was turned half round, perhaps to say darling, or what are you doing. At the very same moment, my mother was coming from the farmyard with two empty buckets. My mother was always carrying buckets, always busy, always modest, and was now about to witness the most profane scene – the half-naked curate and Nancy laughing. Nancy bent and said something to his back, and then they must have heard my mother in the kitchen because suddenly he was putting his shirt on and she was leaving the room. I do not know what she said to him or what caused him to undress. All I know is that I realised she had some secret with men, and that it was a secret that I would never grasp, and never quite understand.

The third woman, Mrs Keogh, did not set foot in our house ever, being too shy. She came once a week, Fridays, after she had drawn her pension, and sat on the back step and drank a cup of buttermilk. She wore heavy serge clothes, the same ones winter and summer, and the same brown velours hat with the two hatpins, one being a huge dented pearl and the other of false emerald stones, many of which were missing. There were holes where the stones should be. She lived across the fields from us and only saw civilisation on Sundays, when she went to Mass, and on Fridays, when she drew her old-age pension. She would sit on the back step and say eagerly to my mother, 'Any news?' She had a habit of lifting her face and the tip of her nose, as if she were a bird about to take off into the air. If she saw my father or a workman coming towards the house, she would run off and leave the unfinished buttermilk. There was seldom any news, and yet she would ask and ask, as if she could be told something that would fill her up until the next week.

She suffered from shingles. She said she hoped that my mother would never get shingles, and in a strange way my mother knew that one day she would. It was as if, out of consolation, one person eventually got another person's ailment, and what they all dreaded getting, was cancer.

Mrs Keogh had only two ambitions in her life, and we knew them. The first was that her husband might be persuaded to build a new house up near the main road, so that she could see people as they went by. All she wanted was to see them and to see whom they were with, and to see what kind of bicycles they rode, or to see the occasional motorcar. Motorcars were still a novelty, and she expressed a great fear of them – said they were dangerous bulls and could easily get out of hand. My mother said nonsense and that they had brakes, just like a bicycle, but we were all vastly ignorant of their workings. One man carried his toolbox on the running board of his car, and it was said to be crammed with implements. Mrs Keogh said to just imagine how many things could go wrong with a car, and my mother said that they need not worry, as it would be Shanks' mare for them until they died. Her second wish – and this was a terrible secret – was that her husband would die before her. In that way, she imagined she could also achieve her first wish. She thought she would sell the house to people with young children and, being a widow, she might get a county-council cottage and grow flowers in a window box. She told this only one time, when she was wracked with pain and was discussing with my mother a new ointment. The ointment was in a little round box, and together they smelled it and were dubious about it. She lifted her bodice and there we saw, like stigmata, a huge crop of sores, and while we were looking at them the terrible wish tumbled out of her mouth and she retracted it at once.

Her life had no variety. They said the Rosary every evening after their tea. They were in bed while it was still bright in summer, and she was up at five or six washing. She was a powerful washer. She washed tables, chairs, the milk tankard, she washed the out-houses, she washed the windows and the sills of windows, and she would have washed the roof of the hay-shed if she had had a ladder long enough. She disliked cooking, and her standby was potatoes, bacon, and cabbage, and nothing else.

Their dogs were savages, so one did not venture there unless it was an emergency. After she had been missing from Mass, my mother and I set out to call on her one Sunday evening. As we came up the overgrown lane that led to their cement house, two ferocious creatures came bounding over the fields, barking and snarling. When we saw that the distance between us and them was desperately shortening we backed away and jumped over a fence, capsizing the uppermost loose plank. They were upon us – two mangy creatures, baring their teeth, so that we could see their torn gums. My mother told me to pick up a stone, and while I did she pushed them backward with the plank, making sure that at least the fence was between our feet and their carnivorousness. Pelting them with sod and stones made them worse, and had not Mrs Keogh's son, Patrick, come to call them we would have been eaten to death. He dragged them away, and still they snarled and still they conspired to get back to us and have their revenge. He did not invite us in.

Mrs Keogh came down the field in a man's hat. She always kept her head covered because of the shingles, and the air could never get to her scalp. Wiping her hands on her apron, she then shook hands with us and begged us to sit down on the loose wall. She did not dare ask us in, as her husband was moody and talked only to the sheep and never kept his money anywhere but under his mattress. He thought that any visitors would be apt to steal or borrow from him.

Mrs Keogh and my mother talked about a new motorcar that Mrs Sparling had got; they raved about it. There were six motorcars in the neighbourhood, but Mrs Sparling's was unique. It was a French car, and she had been given it as a gift by her brothers in America. Her brothers owned big stores there and gave employment to lots of local people who emigrated. My mother said that Mrs Sparling had been born with a silver spoon in her mouth and had kept it there ever since. The car was dark purple, almost maroon, with huge headlamps that gave off two lights, a bright-yellow light and a dimmer, smokier light. I myself had written my name in dust on the bonnet, the day Mrs Sparling, the proud owner, had come to show it off. I had sat in it; I had touched and smelled the red leather seats; I had wielded the steering wheel and zanily imagined going this way and that; I had inadvisedly blown the horn and sent my father's horses into a frenzy. I put my initials on the dusty metal and thought how in a sense I would be travelling all over the countryside.

Mrs Keogh asked about the car in such detail – how big it was, how many could fit comfortably, and if when it was moving the guts and stomach rumbled. We could not answer these things, because we had not driven in it, though of course we aspired to. By way of apologising for not asking us in, she slipped me half-a-crown and from under her skirt produced a carnival jug for my mother. It was a beautiful orange colour and it was almost opaque; yet when my mother held it up in the sunset it gleamed and caught fire. It was like something from a far-off bazaar and completely unlike the dreariness of the surroundings. There were the big piles of cloud, the ragged fields, the hazel trees with their unripe green-skinned nuts, and the little stream that seemed to say tra-la-la tra-la-la tra-la-la.

Thrilled by the gift, my mother made a rash promise. She said that she would ask Mrs Sparling if we could all go for a drive. It was as if the request had been magically made and magically answered, because Mrs Keogh jumped up in excitement, gushed like the stream, and asked what would she wear and when would it be.

As we walked home, my mother regretted her promise, because Mrs Sparling was a snob and made fun of Mrs Keogh, with her long idiotic clothes, her birdlike snout, and her nervous singsong voice. Called her a Mohawk. My mother said she would not ask just yet; she would bide her time. It was because of that we had to start avoiding Mrs Keogh. We had to hide when we saw her coming across the fields on Friday, and after Mass my mother rushed out at the last Gospel, before the rest of the congregation. Mrs Keogh never left the chapel until the throng went out, and so it was easy enough to avoid her. It bothered us one day when she left a sweater on the back step. It was wrapped in old newspaper. It was a beautiful sweater, with a special zigzag pattern, and it must have taken her weeks to knit. It was for me. It had many colours and reminded me of Joseph and the dream coat. Yet getting it put us under an obligation, and I could only enjoy it in spasms.

It was a few weeks later that we heard how Mrs Keogh was seen in the village, in the forester's car, and that she was waving to everyone as they sped by. They went through the village, past the school, and down the very steep hill that led to the lower road, and we learned that they stopped in the next village and went into the lovely hotel with the pale-green walls, green blinds, and, on the veranda, green glass-topped tables and green bamboo chairs. To our astonishment, Mrs Keogh and the forester took a cup of tea in there and Mrs Keogh had the clientele in stitches describing the drive, describing how hedges and houses slid past, saying that it was too quick, was like seeing the tail of a fox as he vanished. Then the forester – he was a distant relation of hers – bought a box of matches, counted them, found there were four missing, reluctantly paid for the two teas, and rose to go home.

At the gateway that led to their little stile, and thence led to a walk across four fields, Mrs Keogh was loath to leave him. She even suggested going to the village, where he lodged, and walking home. He could only get rid of her with the guarantee that he would bring her out again. As she crossed the fields, she took off her hat and coat. She and her husband and son always did that. They would always be stripped of their good clothes by the time they got to the house, so that they could start work straightaway. She hurried in to put on the kettle, to get the feed for the hens, to oil and light the lamp, while gabbing to her son about the drive, her vertigo, the way the car swerved at a very bad corner, the forester's presence of mind. Then all of a sudden she dropped the cup with which she was filling the kettle and said she must go out, as she felt dizzy.

Outside, she stood under the hazel tree and clung to a bough, lowered her head onto it and, without a word, slouched down until her feet had given way, and softly fell and died. There was a seraphic smile on her face, as if the car ride had been the crowning joy of her life. It was what everyone remarked on when they sat in the downstairs room and looked at her remains. Perhaps they found solace in it. I myself could not help thinking of the evening when we sat on the loose wall and the clouds heaved dully by and the little giddy stream went tra-la-la. It was November now, the squirrels had eaten the hazelnuts and the husks were trampled into the ground and were rotting and nourishing the earth. I could not imagine her dead. I still can't. I still can't imagine any of them dead. They live on; they are fixed in that far-off region called childhood, where nothing ever dies, not even oneself.

Sister Imelda

Sister Imelda did not take classes on her first day back in the convent but we spotted her in the grounds after the evening Rosary. Excitement and curiosity impelled us to follow her and try and see what she looked like, but she thwarted us by walking with head bent and eyelids down. All we could be certain of, was that she was tall and limber and that she prayed while she walked. No looking at nature for her, or no curiosity about seventy boarders in gaberdine coats and black shoes and stockings. We might just as well have been crows, so impervious was she to our stares and to abortive attempts at trying to say 'Hello Sister'.

We had returned from our long summer holiday and we were all wretched. The convent with its high stone wall and green iron gates enfolding us again, seeming more of a prison than ever – for after our spell in the outside world we all felt very much older and more sophisticated, and my friend Baba and I were dreaming of our final escape, which would be in a year. And so, on that damp autumn evening when I saw the chrysanthemums and saw the new nun intent on prayer I pitied her and thought how alone she must be, cut off from her friends and conversation with only God as her intangible spouse.

The next day she came into our classroom to take Geometry. Her pale, slightly long face I saw as formidable but her eyes were different, being blue-black and full of verve. Her lips were very purple as if she had put puce pencil on them. They were the lips of a woman who might sing in cabaret and unconsciously she had formed the habit of turning them inwards as if she too was aware of their provocativeness. She had spent the last four years – the same span that Baba and I had spent in the convent – at the university in Dublin where she studied languages. We couldn't understand how she had resisted the temptations of the hectic world and willingly come back to this. Her spell in the outside world made her different from the other nuns, there was more bounce in her walk, more excitement in the way she tackled teaching, reminding us that it was the most important thing in the world as she uttered the phrase 'Praise be the Incarnate World'. She began each day's class by reading from Cardinal Newman who was a favourite of hers. She read how God dwelt in light unapproachable, and how with Him there was neither change nor shadow of alteration. It was amazing how her looks changed. Some days when her eyes were flashing she looked almost profane and made me wonder what events inside the precincts of the convent caused her to be suddenly so excited. She might have been a girl going to a dance except for her habit.

'Hasn't she wonderful eyes,' I said to Baba. That particular day they were like blackberries, large and soft and shiny.

'Something wrong in her upstairs department,' Baba said and added that with make-up Imelda would be a cinch.

'Still she has a vocation!' I said and even aired the idiotic view that I might have one. At certain moments it did seem enticing to become a nun, to lead a life unspotted by sin, never to have to have babies and to wear a ring that singled one out as the Bride of Christ. But there was the other side to it, the silence, the gravity of it, having to get up two or three times a night to pray and above all never having the opportunity of leaving the confines of the place except for the funeral of one's parents. For us boarders it was torture but for the nuns it was nothing short of doom. Also we could complain to each other and we did, food being the source of the greatest grumbles. Lunch was either bacon and cabbage or a peculiar stringy meat followed by tapioca pudding; tea consisted of bread dolloped with lard and occasionally, as a treat, fairly green rhubarb jam, which did not have enough sugar. Through the long curtainless

windows we saw the conifer trees and a sky that was scarcely
ever without the promise of rain or a downpour.

She was a right lunatic then, Baba said, having gone to
university for four years and willingly come back to incarcera-
tion, to poverty, chastity and obedience. We concocted scenes
of agony in some Dublin hostel, while a boy, or even a young
man, stood beneath her bedroom window throwing up chunks
of clay or whistles or a supplication. In our version of it he was
slightly older than her, and possibly a medical student since
medical students had a knack with women, because of studying
diagrams and skeletons. His advances, like those of a sudden
storm would intermittently rise and overwhelm her and the
memory of these sudden flaying advances of his, would haunt
her until she died, and if ever she contracted fever these secrets
would out. It was also rumoured that she possessed a fierce
temper and that while a postulant she had hit a girl so badly with
her leather strap that the girl had to be put to bed because of
wounds. Yet another black mark against Sister Imelda was that
her brother Ambrose had been sued by a nurse for breach of
promise.

That first morning when she came into our classroom and
modestly introduced herself I had no idea how terribly she
would infiltrate my life, how in time she would be not just one of
those teachers or nuns, but rather a special one almost like a
ghost who passed the boundaries of common exchange and who
crept inside one, devouring so much of one's thoughts, so much
of one's passion, invading the place that was called one's heart.
She talked in a low voice as if she did not want her words to go
beyond the bounds of the wall and constantly she stressed the
value of work both to enlarge the mind and discipline the
thought. One of her eyelids was red and swollen as if she was
getting a sty. I reckoned that she over-mortified herself by not
eating at all. I saw in her some terrible premonition of sacrifice
which I would have to emulate. Then in direct contrast she
absently held the stick of chalk between her first and second
fingers the very same as if it were a cigarette and Baba whispered

to me that she might have been a smoker when in Dublin. Sister Imelda looked down sharply at me and said what was the secret and would I like to share it since it seemed so comical. I said 'Nothing Sister, nothing', and her dark eyes yielded such vehemence that I prayed she would never have occasion to punish me.

November came and the tiled walls of the recreation hall oozed moisture and gloom. Most girls had sore throats and were told to suffer this inconvenience to mortify themselves in order to lend a glorious hand in that communion of spirit that linked the living with the dead. It was the month of the Suffering Souls in Purgatory, and as we heard of their twofold agony, the yearning for Christ and the ferocity of the leaping flames that burnt and charred their poor limbs, we were asked to make acts of mortification. Some girls gave up jam or sweets and some gave up talking and so in recreation time they were like dummies making signs with thumb and finger to merely say 'How are you?' Baba said that saner people were locked in the lunatic asylum which was only a mile away. We saw them in the grounds, pacing back and forth, with their mouths agape and dribble coming out of them, like icicles. Among our many fears was that one of those lunatics would break out and head straight for the convent and assault some of the girls.

Yet in the thick of all these dreads I found myself becoming dreadfully happy. I had met Sister Imelda outside of class a few times and I felt that there was an attachment between us. Once it was in the grounds when she did a reckless thing. She broke off a chrysanthemum and offered it to me to smell. It had no smell or at least only something faint that suggested autumn and feeling this to be the case herself she said it was not a gardenia was it. Another time we met in the chapel porch and as she drew her shawl more tightly around her body I felt how human she was, and prey to the cold.

In the classroom things were not so congenial between us. Geometry was my worst subject and indeed a total mystery to me. She had not taken more than four classes when she realised this and threw a duster at me in a rage. A few girls gasped as she

asked me to stand up and make a spectacle of myself. Her face
had reddened and presently she took out her handkerchief and
patted the eye which was red and swollen. I not only felt a fool
but I felt in imminent danger of sneezing as I inhaled the smell
of chalk that had fallen onto my gym-frock. Suddenly she fled
from the room leaving us ten minutes free until the next class.
Some girls said it was a disgrace, said I should write home and
say I had been assaulted. Others welcomed the few minutes in
which to gabble. All I wanted was to run after her and say that I
was sorry to have caused her such distemper because I knew
dimly that it was as much to do with liking as it was with dislike.
In me then there came a sort of speechless tenderness for her
and I might have known that I was stirred.

'We could get her de-frocked,' Baba said and elbowed me
in God's name to sit down.

That evening at Benediction I had the most overwhelming
surprise. It was a particularly happy evening with the choir
nuns in full soaring form and the rows of candles like so many
little ladders to the golden chalice that glittered all the more
because of the beams of fitful flame. I was full of tears when I
discovered a new holy picture had been put in my prayer book
and before I dared look on the back to see who had given it to me
I felt and guessed that this was no ordinary picture from an
ordinary girl friend, that this was a talisman and a peace offering
from Sister Imelda. It was a pale-blue picture so pale that it was
almost grey like the down of a pigeon and it showed a mother
looking down on the infant child. On the back, in her beautiful
ornate handwriting, she had written a verse:

> *Trust Him when dark doubts assail thee,*
> *Trust Him when thy faith is small,*
> *Trust Him when to simply trust Him*
> *Seems the hardest thing of all.*

This was her atonement. To think that she had located the
compartment in the chapel where I kept my prayer book and to
think that she had been so naked as to write in it and give me a
chance to boast about it and to show it to other girls. When

I thanked her next day she bowed but did not speak. Mostly the nuns were on silence and only permitted to talk during class.

In no time I had received another present, a little miniature prayer book with a leather cover and gold edging. The prayers were in French and the lettering so minute it was as if a tiny insect had fashioned them. Soon I was publicly known as her pet. I opened doors for her, raised the blackboard two pegs higher (she was taller than other nuns) and handed out the exercise books which she had corrected. Now, in the margins of my geometry propositions I would find 'Good' or 'Excellent', when in the past she used to splash 'Disgraceful'. Baba said it was foul to be a nun's pet and that any girl who sucked up to a nun could not be trusted.

About a month later Sister Imelda asked me to carry her books up four flights of stairs to the cookery kitchen. She taught cookery to a junior class. As she walked ahead of me I thought how supple she was and how thoroughbred and when she paused on the landing to look out through the long curtainless window, I too paused. Down below two women in suede boots were chatting and smoking as they moved down the street with shopping baskets. Nearby a lay nun was down on her knees scrubbing the granite steps and the cold air was full of the smell of raw Jeyes Fluid. There was a potted plant on the landing and Sister Imelda put her fingers in the earth and went 'tch tch tch', saying it needed water. I said I would water it later on. I was happy in my prison then, happy to be near her, happy to walk behind her as she twirled her beads and bowed to the servile nun. I no longer cried for my mother, no longer counted the days on a pocket calendar, until the Christmas holidays.

'Come back at five,' she said as she stood on the threshold of the cookery kitchen door. The girls all in white overalls were arraigned around the long wooden table waiting for her. It was as if every girl was in love with her. Because, as she entered, their faces broke into smiles and in different tones of audacity they said her name. She must have liked cookery class because

she beamed and called to someone, anyone, to get up a blazing
fire. Then she went across to the cast-iron stove and spat on it to
test its temperature. It was hot because her spit rose up and
sizzled.

When I got back later she was sitting on the edge of the
table swaying her legs. There was something reckless about her
pose, something defiant. It seemed as if any minute she would
take out a cigarette case, snap it open and then archly offer me
one. The wonderful smell of baking made me realise how
hungry I was, but far more so, it brought back to me my own
home, my mother testing orange cakes with a knitting needle
and letting me lick the line of half-baked dough down the length
of the needle. I wondered if she had supplanted my mother and
I hoped not, because I had aimed to outstep my original world
and take my place in a new and hallowed one.

'I bet you have a sweet tooth,' she said and then she got up,
crossed the kitchen and from under a wonderful shining silver
cloche she produced two jam tarts with a criss-cross design on
them, where the pastry was latticed over the dark jam. They
were still warm.

'What will I do with them?' I asked.

'Eat them, you goose,' she said and she watched me eat as
if she herself derived some peculiar pleasure from it whereas I
was embarrassed about the pastry crumbling and the bits of
blackberry jam staining the lips. She was amused. It was one of
the most awkward yet thrilling moments I had lived, and inher-
ent in the pleasure was the terrible sense of danger. Had we
been caught she, no doubt, would have to make massive
sacrifice. I looked at her and thought how peerless and how
brave and I wondered if she felt hungry. She had a white overall
over her black habit and this made her warmer, freer, and
caused me to think of the happiness that would be ours, the
laissez-faire if we were away from the convent in an ordinary
kitchen doing something easy and customary. But we weren't.
It was clear to me then that my version of pleasure was inextric-
able from pain and they existed side by side and were inter-
dependent like the two forces of an electric current.

'Had you a friend when you were in Dublin at university?'
I asked daringly.

'I shared a desk with a sister from Howth and stayed in the
same hostel,' she said.

'But what about boys?' I thought, 'and what of your life
now and do you long to go out into the world?' But could not say
it.

We knew something about the nuns' routine. It was
rumoured that they wore itchy, wool underwear, ate dry bread
for breakfast, rarely had meat, cakes or dainties, kept certain
hours of strict silence with each other, as well as constant vigil
on their thoughts; so that if their minds wandered to the subject
of food or pleasure they would quickly revert to thoughts of God
and their eternal souls. They slept on hard beds with no sheets
and hairy blankets. At four o'clock in the morning while we
slept, each nun got out of bed, in her habit – which was also her
death habit – and, chanting, they all flocked down the wooden
stairs like ravens, to fling themselves on the tiled floor of the
chapel. Each nun – even the Mother Superior – flung herself in
total submission, saying prayers in Latin and offering up the
moment to God. Then silently back to their cells for one more
hour of rest. It was not difficult to imagine Sister Imelda face
downwards, arms outstretched, prostrate on the tiled floor. I
often heard their chanting when I wakened suddenly from a
nightmare, because, although we slept in a different building,
both adjoined, and if one wakened one often heard that mono-
tonous Latin chanting, long before the birds began, long before
our own bell summoned us to rise at six.

'Do you eat nice food?' I asked.

'Of course,' she said and smiled. She sometimes broke into
an eager smile which she did much to conceal.

'Have you ever thought of what you will be?' she
asked.

I shook my head. My design changed from day to
day.

She looked at her man's silver pocket watch, closed
the damper of the range and prepared to leave. She checked that

all the wall presses were locked by running her hand over them.

'Sister,' I called, gathering enough courage at last. We must have some secret, something to join us together, 'What colour hair have you?'

We never saw the nuns' hair, or their eyebrows, or ears, as all that part was covered by a stiff, white guimp.

'You shouldn't ask such a thing,' she said, getting pink in the face, and then she turned back and whispered, 'I'll tell you on your last day here, provided your geometry has improved.'

She had scarcely gone when Baba, who had been lurking behind some pillar, stuck her head in the door and said 'Christ sake save me a bit.' She finished the second pastry, then went around looking in kitchen drawers. Because of everything being locked she found only some castor sugar in a china shaker. She ate a little and threw the remainder into the dying fire so that it flared up for a minute with a yellow spluttering flame. Baba showed her jealousy by putting it around the school that I was in the cookery kitchen every evening, gorging cakes with Sister Imelda and telling tales.

I did not speak to Sister Imelda again in private until the evening of our Christmas theatricals. She came to help us put on make-up and get into our stage clothes and fancy headgears. These clothes were kept in a trunk from one year to the next and though sumptuous and though strewn with braiding and gold they smelt of camphor. Yet as we donned them we felt different and as we sponged pancake make-up onto our faces we became saucy and emphasised these new guises by adding dark pencil to the eyes and making the lips bright orange. There was only one tube of lipstick and each girl clamoured for it. The evening's entertainment was to comprise scenes from Shakespeare and laughing sketches. I had been chosen to recite Mark Antony's lament over Caesar's body and for this I was to wear a purple toga, white knee-length socks and patent buckle shoes. The shoes were too big and I moved in them as if in clogs. She said to take them off, to go barefoot. I realised that I was getting nervous and that in an effort to memorise my speech the words were getting all askew and flying about in my head, like the separate pieces of a jigsaw puzzle. She sensed my panic and very slowly put her hand on my face and enjoined me to look at her. I looked into her eyes which seemed fathomless and saw that she was willing me to be calm and obliging me to be master of my fears and I little knew that one day she would have to do the same as regards the swoop of my feelings for her. As we continued to stare I felt myself becoming calm and the words were restored to me in their right and fluent order. The lights were being lowered out in the recreation hall and we knew now that all the nuns had arrived, had settled themselves down and were eagerly awaiting this annual hotchpotch of amateur entertainment. There was that fearsome hush as the hall went dark and the few spotlights turned on. She kissed her crucifix and I realised that she was saying a prayer for me. Then she raised her arm as if depicting the stance of a Greek goddess and walking onto the stage I was fired by her ardour.

Baba could say that I bawled like a bloody bull but Sister Imelda who stood in the wings said that temporarily she had felt the streets of Rome had seen the corpse of Caesar as I delivered those poignant, distempered lines. When I came off stage she put her arms around me and I was encased in a shower of silent kisses. After we had taken down the decorations and put the fancy clothes back in the trunk, I gave her two half-pound boxes of chocolates – bought for me illicitly by one of the day-girls – and she gave me a casket made from the insides of match boxes and covered over with gilt paint and gold dust. It was like holding moths and finding their powder adhering to the fingers.

'What will you do on Christmas Day, Sister?' I said.

'I'll pray for you,' she said.

It was useless to say 'Will you have turkey?' or 'Will you have plum pudding?' or 'Will you loll in bed?', because I believed that Christmas Day would be as bleak and deprived as any other day in her life. Yet she was radiant as if such austerity was joyful. Maybe she was basking in some secret realisation involving her and me.

On the cold snowy afternoon three weeks later when we returned from our holidays Sister Imelda came up to the dormitory to welcome me back. All the other girls had gone down to the recreation hall to do barn dances and I could hear someone banging on the piano. I did not want to go down and clump around with sixty other girls, having nothing to look forward to, only tea and the Rosary and early bed. The beds were damp after our stay at home and when I put my hand between the sheets it was like feeling dew but did not have the freshness of outdoors. What depressed me further was that I had seen a mouse in one of the cupboards, seen its tail curl with terror as it slipped away into a crevice. If there was one mouse, there was God knows how many, and the cakes we hid in secret would not be safe. I was still unpacking as she came down the narrow passage between the rows of iron beds and I saw in her walk such agitation.

'Tut, tut, tut, you've curled your hair,' she said, offended.

Yes, the world outside was somehow declared in this perm and for a second I remembered the scalding pain as the trickles of ammonia dribbled down my forehead and then the joy as the hairdresser said that she would make me look like Movita, a Mexican star. Now suddenly that world and those aspirations seemed trite and I wanted to take a brush and straighten my hair and revert to the dark gawky sombre girl that I had been. I offered her iced queen cakes that my mother had made but she refused them and said she could only stay a second. She lent me a notebook of hers, which she had had as a pupil, and into which she had copied favourite quotations, some religious, some not. I read at random:

> *Twice or thrice had I loved thee*
> *Before I knew thy face or name*
> *So in a voice, so in a shapeless flame*
> *Angels affect us oft.*

'Are you well?' I asked.

She looked pale. It may have been the day, which was wretched and grey with sleet or it may have been the white bedspreads but she appeared to be ailing.

'I missed you,' she said.

'Me too,' I said.

At home, gorging, eating trifle at all hours, even for breakfast, having little ratafias to dip in cups of tea, fitting on new shoes and silk stockings, I wished that she could be with us, enjoying the fire and the freedom.

'You know it is not proper for us to be so friendly.'

'It's not wrong,' I said.

I dreaded that she might decide to turn away from me, that she might stamp on our love and might suddenly draw a curtain over it, a black crêpe curtain that would denote its death. I dreaded it and knew it was going to happen.

'We must not become attached,' she said and I could not say we already were, no more than I could remind her of the day of the revels and the intimacy between us. Convents were dungeons and no doubt about it.

From then on she treated me as less of a favourite. She said my name sharply in class and once she said if I must cough could I wait until class had finished. Baba was delighted as were the other girls because they were glad to see me receding in her eyes. Yet I knew that that crispness was part of her love because no matter how callously she looked at me, she would occasionally soften. Reading her notebook helped me and I copied out her quotations into my own book, trying as accurately as possible to imitate her handwriting.

But some little time later when she came to supervise our study one evening I got a smile from her as she sat on the rostrum looking down at us all. I continued to look up at her and by slight frowning indicated that I had a problem with my geometry. She beckoned to me lightly and I went up bringing my copybook and the pen. Standing close to her, and also because her guimp was crooked, I saw one of her eyebrows for the first time. She saw that I noticed it and said did that satisfy my curiosity. I said not really. She said what else did I want to see, her swan's neck perhaps, and I went scarlet. I was amazed that she would say such a thing in the hearing of other girls and then she said a worse thing, she said that G. K. Chesterton was very forgetful and had once put on his trousers backwards. She expected me to laugh. I was so close to her that a rumble in her stomach seemed to be taking place in my own and about this she also laughed. It occurred to me for one terrible moment that maybe she had decided to leave the convent to jump over the wall. Having done the theorem for me she marked it 'one hundred out of one hundred' and then asked if I had any other problems. My eyes filled with tears as I wanted her to realise that her recent coolness had wrought havoc with my nerves and my peace of mind.

'What is it?' she said.

I could cry or I could tremble to try and convey the emotion but I could not tell her. As if on cue, the Mother Superior came in, and saw this glaring intimacy and frowned as she approached the rostrum.

'Would you please go back to your desk,' she said, 'and in future kindly allow Sister Imelda to get on with her duties.'

I tiptoed back and sat with head down, bursting with fear and shame. Then she looked at a tray on which the milk cups were laid and finding one cup of milk untouched she asked which girl had not drunk her milk.

'Me, Sister,' I said, and I was called up to drink it and stand under the clock as a punishment. The milk was tepid and dusty and I thought of cows on the fairs days at home and the farmers hitting them as they slid and slithered over the muddy streets.

For weeks I tried to see my nun in private and I even lurked outside doors where I knew she was due, only to be rebuffed again and again. I suspected the Mother Superior had warned her against making a favourite of me. But I still clung to a belief that a bond existed between us and that her coldness and even some glares which I had received were a charade, a mask. I would wonder how she felt alone in bed and what way she slept and if she thought of me, or refusing to think of me if she dreamt of me as I did of her. She certainly got thinner because her nun's silver ring slipped easily and sometimes unavoidably off her marriage finger. It occurred to me that she was having a nervous breakdown.

One day in March the sun came out, the radiators were turned off, and though there was a lashing wind we were told that officially Spring had arrived, and that we could play games. We all trooped up to the games field and to our surprise, saw that Sister Imelda was officiating that day. The daffodils in the field tossed and turned and they were a very bright shocking yellow but they were not as fetching as the little timid snowdrops that trembled in the wind. We played rounders and when my turn came to hit the ball with the long wooden pound I crumbled and missed, fearing that the ball would hit me.

'Champ . . .' said Baba jeering.

After three such failures Sister Imelda said that if I liked I could sit and watch, and when I was sitting in the greenhouse swallowing my shame she came in and said that I must not give way to tears because humiliation was the greatest test of Christ's love or indeed *any* love.

'When you are a nun you will know that,' she said and instantly I made up my mind that I would be a nun and that though we might never be free to express our feelings we would be under the same roof, in the same cloister, in mental and spiritual conjunction all our lives.

'Is it very hard at first?' I said.

'It's awful,' she said and she slipped a little medal into my gym frock pocket. It was warm from being in her pocket and as I held it, I knew that once again we were near and that in fact we had never severed. Walking down from the playing field to our Sunday lunch of mutton and cabbage everyone chattered to Sister Imelda. The girls milled around her, linking her, trying to hold her hand, counting the various keys on her bunch of keys and asking impudent questions.

'Sister, did you ever ride a motor bicycle?'

'Sister, did you ever wear seamless stockings?'

'Sister, who's your favourite film star – male!'

'Sister, what's your favourite food?'

'Sister, if you had a wish what would it be?'

'Sister, what do you do when you want to scratch your head?'

Yes, she had ridden a motor bicycle, and she had worn silk stockings but they were seamed. She liked bananas best and if she had a wish it would be to go home for a few hours to see her parents, and her brother.

That afternoon as we walked through the town the sight of closed shops with porter barrels outside, and mongrel dogs did not dispel my re-found ecstasy. The medal was in my pocket and every other second I would touch it for confirmation. Baba saw a Swiss roll in a confectioner's window laid on a doily and dusted with caster sugar and its appeal made her cry out with hunger, and rail against being in a bloody reformatory, surrounded by drips and mopes. On impulse she took her nail file out of her pocket and dashed across to the window to see if she could cut the glass. The prefect rushed up from the back of the line and asked Baba if she wanted to be locked up.

'I am anyhow,' Baba said and sawed at one of her nails, to maintain her independence and vent her spleen. Baba was the only girl who could stand up to a prefect. When she felt like it she dropped out of a walk, sat on a stone wall and waited until we all came back. She said that if there was one thing more boring than studying it was walking. She used to roll down her stockings and examine her calves and say that she could see varicose veins coming from this bloody daily walk. Her legs like all our legs were black from the dye of the stockings and we were forbidden to bathe because baths were immoral. We washed each night in an enamel basin beside our beds. When girls splashed cold water onto their chests they let out cries, though this was forbidden.

After the walk we wrote home. We were allowed to write home once a week; our letters were always censored. I told my mother that I had made up my mind to be a nun, and asked if she could send me bananas, when a batch arrived at our local grocery shop. That evening, perhaps as I wrote to my mother on the ruled white paper, a telegram arrived which said that Sister Imelda's brother had been killed in a van, while on his way home from a hurling match. The Mother Superior announced it, and asked us to pray for his soul and write letters of sympathy to Sister Imelda's parents. We all wrote identical letters, because in our first year at school we had been given specimen letters for various occasions, and we all referred back to our specimen letter of sympathy.

Next day the town hire-car drove up to the convent and Sister Imelda, accompanied by another nun, went home for the funeral. She looked as white as a sheet with eyes swollen and she wore a heavy knitted shawl over her shoulders. Although she came back that night (I stayed awake to hear the car) we did not see her for a whole week, except to catch a glimpse of her back, in the chapel. When she resumed class she was peaky and distant, making no reference at all to her recent tragedy.

The day the bananas came I waited outside the door and gave her a bunch wrapped in tissue paper. Some were still a little green, and she said that Mother Superior would put them in the glasshouse to ripen. I felt that Sister Imelda would never taste them; they would be kept for a visiting priest or bishop.

'Oh Sister, I'm sorry about your brother,' I said, in a burst.

'It will come to us all, sooner or later,' Sister Imelda said dolefully.

I dared to touch her wrist to communicate my sadness. She went quickly, probably for fear of breaking down. At times she grew irritable and had a boil on her cheek. She missed some classes and was replaced in the cookery kitchen by a younger nun. She asked me to pray for her brother's soul and to avoid seeing her alone. Each time as she came down a corridor towards me I was obliged to turn the other way. Now, Baba or some other girl moved the blackboard two pegs higher and spread her shawl, when wet, over the radiator to dry.

I got 'flu and was put to bed. Sickness took the same bleak course, a cup of hot senna delivered in person by the head-nun who stood there while I drank it, tea at lunch-time with thin slices of brown bread (because it was just after the war food was still rationed, so the butter was mixed with lard and had white streaks running through it and a faintly rancid smell), hours of just lying there surveying the empty dormitory, the empty iron beds with white counterpanes on each one, and metal crucifixes laid on each white, frilled, pillow-slip. I knew that she would miss me and hoped that Baba would tell her where I was. I counted the number of tiles from the ceiling to the head of my bed, thought of my mother at home on the farm mixing hen food, thought of my father, losing his temper perhaps and stamping on the kitchen floor with nailed boots and I recalled the money owing for my school fees and hoped that Sister Imelda would never get to hear of it. During the Christmas holiday I had seen a bill sent by the head-nun to my father which said, 'Please remit this week without fail.' I hated being in bed causing extra trouble and therefore reminding the head-nun of the unpaid liability. We had no clock in the dormitory, so there was no way of guessing the time, but the hours dragged.

Marigold, one of the maids, came to take off the counterpanes at five and brought with her two gifts from Sister Imelda – an orange and a pencil sharpener. I kept the orange peel in my hand, smelling it, and planning how I would thank her. Thinking of her I fell into a feverish sleep and was wakened when the girls came to bed at ten and switched on the various ceiling lights.

At Easter Sister Imelda warned me not to give her chocolates so I got her a flashlamp instead and spare batteries. Pleased with such a useful gift (perhaps she read her letters in bed), she put her arms round me and allowed one cheek to adhere but not to make the sound of a kiss. It made up for the seven weeks of withdrawal, and as I drove down the convent drive with Baba she waved to me, as she had promised, from the window of her cell.

In the last term at school studying was intensive because of the examinations which loomed at the end of June. Like all the other nuns Sister Imelda thought only of these examinations. She crammed us with knowledge, lost her temper every other day and gritted her teeth whenever the blackboard was too greasy to take the imprint of the chalk. If ever I met her in the corridor she asked if I knew such and such a thing, and coming down from Sunday games she went over various questions with us. The fateful examination day arrived and we sat at single desks supervised by some strange woman from Dublin. Opening a locked trunk she took out the pink examination papers and distributed them around. Geometry was on the fourth day. When we came out from it, Sister Imelda was in the hall with all the answers, so that we could compare our answers with hers. Then she called me aside and we went up towards the cookery kitchen and sat on the stairs while she went over the paper with me, question for question. I knew that I had three right and two wrong, but did not tell her so.

'It is black,' she said then, rather suddenly. I thought she meant the dark light where we were sitting.

'It's cool though,' I said.

Summer had come, our white skins baked under the heavy uniform and dark violet pansies bloomed in the convent grounds. She looked well again and her pale skin was once more unblemished.

'My hair,' she whispered, 'is black.' And she told me how she had spent her last night before entering the convent. She had gone cycling with a boy and ridden for miles, and they'd lost their way up a mountain and she became afraid she would be so late home that she would sleep it out next morning. It was understood between us that I was going to enter the convent in September and that I could have a last fling too.

Two days later we prepared to go home. There were farewells and outlandish promises, and autograph books signed, and girls trudging up the recreation hall, their cases bursting open with clothes and books. Baba scattered biscuit crumbs in the dormitory for the mice, and stuffed all her prayer books under a mattress. Her father promised to collect us at four. I had arranged with Sister Imelda secretly that I would meet her in one of the summer houses around the walks, where we would spend our last half-hour together. I expected that she would tell me something of what my life as a postulant would be like. But Baba's father came an hour early. He had something urgent to do later and came at three instead. All I could do was ask Marigold to take a note to Sister Imelda.

> *Remembrance is all I ask,*
> *But if remembrance should prove a task,*
> *Forget me.*

I hated Baba, hated her busy father, hated the thought of my mother standing in the doorway in her good dress, welcoming me home at last. I would have become a nun that minute if I could.

I wrote to my nun that night and again next day and then every week for a month. Her letters were censored so I tried to convey my feelings indirectly. In one of her letters to me (they were allowed one letter a month) she said that she looked forward to seeing me in September. But by September Baba and I had left for the university in Dublin. I stopped writing to Sister Imelda then, reluctant to tell her that I no longer wished to be a nun.

In Dublin we enrolled at the college where she had surpassed herself. I saw her maiden name on a list, for having graduated with special honours, and for days was again sad and remorseful. I rushed out and bought batteries for the flashlamp I'd given her, and posted them without any note enclosed. No mention of my missing vocation, no mention of why I had stopped writing.

One Sunday about two years later Baba and I were going out to Howth on a bus. Baba had met some businessmen who played golf there and she had done a lot of scheming to get us invited out. The bus was packed, mostly mothers with babies and children on their way to Dollymount Strand. We drove along the coast road and saw the sea, bright green and glinting in the sun and because of the way the water was carved up into millions of little wavelets its surface seemed like an endless heap of dark green broken bottles. Near the shore the sand looked warm and was biscuit-coloured. We never swam or sunbathed, we never did anything that was good for us. Life was geared to work and to meeting men and yet one knew that mating could only but lead to one's being a mother and hawking obstreperous children out to the seaside on Sunday. 'They know not what they do' could surely be said of us.

We were very made up and even the conductor seemed to disapprove and snapped at having to give the change of ten shillings. For no reason at all I thought of our make-up rituals before the school play and how innocent it was in comparison because now our skins were smothered beneath layers of it and we never took it off at night. Thinking of the convent I suddenly thought of Sister Imelda and then as if prey to a dream, I heard the rustle of serge, smelt the Jeyes Fluid and the boiled cabbage and saw her pale shocked face in the months after her brother died. Then I looked around and saw her in earnest and at first thought that I was imagining things. But no, she had got on accompanied by another nun and they were settling themselves in the back seat nearest the door. She looked older but she had the same aloof quality and the same eyes and my heart began to race with a mixture of excitement and dread. At first it raced with a prodigal strength and then it began to falter and I thought it was going to give out. My fear of her and my love came back in one fell realisation. I would have gone through the window except that it was not wide enough. The thing was how to escape her. Baba gurgled with delight, stood up and in the most flagrant way looked around to make sure that it was Imelda. She recognised the other nun as one with the nickname of Johnny who taught piano lessons. Baba's first thought was revenge, as she enumerated the punishments they had meted out to us and said how nice it would be to go back and shock them and say 'Mud in your eye, Sisters', or 'Get lost', or something worse. Baba could not understand why I was quaking no more than she could understand why I began to wipe off the lipstick. Above all I knew that I could not confront them.

'You're going to have to,' Baba said.

'I can't,' I said.

It was not just my attire, it was the fact of never having written and of my broken promise. Baba kept looking back and said they weren't saying a word and that children were gawking at them. It wasn't often that nuns travelled in buses and we speculated as to where they might be going.

'They might be off to meet two fellows,' Baba said, and visualised them in the golf club getting blotto and hoisting up their skirts. For me it was no laughing matter. She came up with a strategy and it was that as we approached our stop and the bus was still moving I was to jump up and go down the aisle and pass them without even looking. She said most likely they would not notice us as their eyes were lowered and they seemed to be praying.

'I can't run down the bus,' I said. There was a matter of shaking limbs and already a terrible vertigo.

'You're going to,' Baba said, and though insisting that I couldn't I had already begun to rehearse an apology. While doing this I kept blessing myself over and over again and Baba kept reminding me that there was only one more stop before ours. When the dreadful moment came I jumped up and put on my face what can only be called an apology of a smile. I followed Baba to the rear of the bus. But already they had gone. I saw the back of their two sable, identical figures with their veils being blown wildly about in the wind. They looked so cold and lost as they hurried along the pavement and I wanted to run after them. In some way I felt worse than if I had confronted them. I cannot be certain what I would have said. I knew that there is something sad and faintly distasteful about love's ending, particularly love that has never been fully realised. I might have hinted at that but I doubt it. In our deepest moments we say the most inadequate things.

Also by Edna O'Brien
available in Phoenix paperback

House of Splendid Isolation

When Josie, confined to bed in her dilapidated country mansion, sees the door swing back and the hooded face appear, she knows who it is. Into her world comes McGreevy, bloody crusader for a united Ireland, who has chosen her home for sanctuary. Within the incarcerating walls of the house, an undercurrent of love develops between two people who think differently but feel the same. Destiny has flung them together, and as the police net closes in, fear dawns in Josie that McGreevy has used her house for more than refuge. And there may be no escape for either of them.

Price: £6.99
ISBN: 1 85799 209 1

Down by the River

In the deceptively idyllic setting of rural Ireland, a crime of passion results in an emotional battlefield. At the centre of the crisis, a young girl struggles with the conflicts of mind and body, the teaching of her faith and her mounting bewilderment at what she must do. As she tries to conceal, then escape her fate, she finds herself driven to the brink of despair. And then her private – and redeemable – tragedy is dragged into the public realm, and the power of decision is taken out of her hands.

Price: £6.99
ISBN: 1 85799 873 1

All Orion/Phoenix/Indigo titles are available at your local bookshop or from the following address:

Mail Order Department
Littlehampton Book Services
FREEPOST BR535
Worthing, West Sussex, BN13 3BR
telephone 01903 828503, *facsimile* 01903 828802
e-mail MailOrders@lbsltd.co.uk
(Please ensure that you include full postal address details)

Payment can be made either by credit/debit card (Visa, Mastercard, Access and Switch accepted) or by sending a £ Sterling cheque or postal order made payable to *Littlehampton Book Services*.
DO NOT SEND CASH OR CURRENCY.

Please add the following to cover postage and packing

UK and BFPO:
£1.50 for the first book, and 50p for each additional book to a maximum of £3.50

Overseas and Eire:
£2.50 for the first book plus £1.00 for the second book and 50p for each additional book ordered

- -

BLOCK CAPITALS PLEASE

name of cardholder ....   *delivery address*
                          ....   *(if different from cardholder)*
address of cardholder ....

....

....

    postcode ....   *postcode* ....

☐   I enclose my remittance for £...........................

☐   please debit my Mastercard/Visa/Access/Switch (delete as appropriate)

card number ⬚⬚⬚⬚ ⬚⬚⬚⬚ ⬚⬚⬚⬚ ⬚⬚⬚⬚ ⬚⬚

expiry date ⬚⬚⬚⬚   Switch issue no. ⬚⬚

signature ....

prices and availability are subject to change without notice